Merging
in Minnesota

Merging
in Minnesota

Michael Phillips

Merging in Minnesota

Published by
Lone Oak Publishing
SAN 257-4330
5531 Dufferin Drive
Savage, Minnesota, 55378
United States of America

www.loneoakpublishing.com

Here's what the critics are saying about *Merging in Minnesota* . . . .

"I couldn't put it down . . . well, I had to put it down sometimes, like when I needed to go to the bathroom, or get something to eat, or watch TV... eh, you know what I mean?"
Bill Stevens – The Columbus Trumpeter

"It brought me back to life!"
Christopher Wren – Seventeenth Century Architect

"I give it Five Stars and one of those furry little pink ball things that fasten onto children's mittens!"
Fran Tick – Irvine Gazebo

"I couldn't put it down . . . unlike some people."
Fred Stevens – The Columbus Bugler

"I think the critic reviews at the beginning of the book are funnier than the story."
A. Nonymus – The Cleveland Indian

"It is to muse, but for what gain? It is thy wandering page that maketh me full of outward disdain. And yet I rest with complete serenity under thy comely shadow."
Creative Writing Student from Berkley

"It makes for a nice break from my tortured hell."
A. Camus

"It's a delicious book."
A. Goat

"The pricing is about right."
Pop goes the Weasel

"Outlandish. A total treat for the entire family!"
Roger e-Bert

"Humorous? . . . sometimes . . . sometimes not very much . . . sometimes infrequently . . . ."
Critic Bill Smith mulling it over

"I found I could in fact put it down."
Harry Adams – The Columbus Yodeler

"It's rife with pages!"
Tammy Tipton-Hat – Nashville Trib-Gazzette

"If I see one more joke about stupid fictitious newspapers, I will scream!!!"
Bill Fowler – Washington Post Yodeler

CHAPTER 1

Zeke Martin was a man of simple pleasures. He never expected much from life and so his disappointments were few. He enjoyed having a simple, well-kept home – one that was well-organized, not overwhelmed with clutter and not adorned with overly pretentious items like fancy drapes or furniture.

Zeke's taste in decor was simple as well, with the exception of course being his den. In the den were potted palm trees, bamboo furniture, various stuffed animals such as a tiger and large boar, various antiques such as an eighteenth century chronometer and sextant. It all had the look and feel of an officer's quarters from the British East India Company from the early 1800s.

Zeke noticing the odd allusion to Imperial Great Britain, tried to change things up a bit by including pictures of Elvis Presley – his childhood idol – a Hawaiian hula dancer lamp, and a priceless second century Ming vase. Where he could locate and purchase such an expensive Chinese relic was a mystery to everyone who knew Zeke – especially given the fact that he only made $70,000 a year as a highway investigator for the Department of Transportation. One guest to the den did note that on the bottom of the vase, written in Chinese were the words "Made in China." Needless to say, Zeke Martin was a bit of an eccentric.

Apart from the den which he also referred to as the Jungle-room – in honor of Elvis – Zeke wanted everything else simple. Gloria his wife complained to Zeke continually about this as she usually wanted things as complicated as humanly possible. Gloria was an intellectual and needed to be continually stimulated – and so Zeke ignored Gloria as much as possible.

Zeke's entertainment needs were simple as well. A beer and a good football game on TV were all he required – that and an occasional foray into the basement where he would experiment with Einstein's theory of relativity. His taste in food was also not demanding; meat and potatoes were his staple. And so when Zeke was greeted at home that evening with a plate full of Hamburger Helper, it was a real pleasure he seldom enjoyed. Oh sure, Gloria could rustle up a mean Sloppy Joe or *pâté de foie gras* once in awhile, but to quietly enjoy a plate of Hamburger Helper, especially the Noodle Stroganoff version, was a real treat in the Martin home. When the phone started ringing in the middle of Zeke's meal he was understandably angered by the interruption.

"Zeke! Hank Fargo with the Shakopee police. I need you to come down here ASAP!" screamed the voice at the other end of the phone.

Zeke, still choking down a morsel of Hamburger Helper questioned Fargo's urgency.

"I need you here on the double. We've had a major

accident on highway 169, on the off-ramp which turns into highway 100!"

Zeke put down the phone and begrudgingly headed to the garage, all the while staring at his abandoned plate of Hamburger Helper. He bid Gloria a fond farewell in the form of a grunt and then hopped into his pick-up. His garage, which was a museum of auto-racing, had the walls plastered with posters of his favorite racing teams. His workbench was immaculately stacked with various tool boxes and other sundry Craftsmen paraphernalia. As he quietly warmed up the pick-up, he grinned at the portrait of his father that hung above his workbench.

Zeke's dad was a colorful character who won his fifteen minutes of fame by being a mechanic in Johnny Rutherford's pit crew. During a 1965 race, Billy Martin was hit in the head by a runaway tire that had come lose from one of the stock cars. The injury was severe and required multiple surgeries, eventually requiring that a metal plate be put in his head. This made life difficult for Billy, as the only work he could get post racing accident was as a grinder in an auto parts shop. The metal shavings would immediately stick to his head and he would continually have to wipe them off.

As he backed down the driveway to the nearby street, Zeke waved to his neighbor, Bill Wilson, pulling into his driveway after a long day at work.

Zeke headed into the dark Burnsville night driving slowly as he got onto highway 13. Zeke was a little cautious as he drove into the western part of Burnsville and into the neighboring town of Savage. There was a stretch of highway

13 that made Zeke a bit anxious. It was near where the road started to run by the Minnesota River next to the Fishgill cargo port. Deer were plentiful there and Zeke had to keep an eye out.

Deer were not Zeke's favorite subject of late. He had totaled his other pick-up truck two evenings prior when a deer seemed to pop up in front of him as he made his way to his office. Since moving to Minnesota, Zeke had either killed or badly injured six deer. He mused that he probably had incapacitated more deer than the average Minnesota hunter. In all cases his vehicle had been badly damaged and Zeke had grown to be fearful of these streaking targets. They soon invaded his dreams at night as some sort of mechanical targets in an arcade game – they seemed to literally just pop up like a metal target one shoots at in the fairs or carnivals.

It was no coincidence it seemed when the Regional Director Waxhead assigned Zeke to look into ways to control deer strikes in the southern district that Zeke presided over. It had become a thorn in Zeke's side as he continued to ponder ways of reducing the amount of deer interfering with road traffic. With this assignment the dreams, which were really nightmares, became more frequent. Although an animal lover, owner of three dogs and a cat, the deer population had become his enemy – a mindless dark force that seemed to be attracted to any vehicle he drove.

Despite the deer, Zeke had enjoyed his twenty years in his Burnsville neighborhood. Although a native of Gulfport, Alabama, he gladly moved to Minnesota to fulfill his dream of becoming a Highway Investigator for the Department of Transportation. He had always loved cars as a child, but it was roads and highways that were his true passion. If anyone wanted to know anything about roads, streets, alleys, cul-de-sacs, highways and freeways, Zeke could tell you everything. From the first Roman road built over two millennia ago, to the German autobahn, to the first modern freeway built in Los Angeles in the 1950s, Zeke could tell you every aspect of each project down to the first name of the chief engineer.

Zeke had studied highway sciences at the University of Coastal Alabama, minoring in rubber tire physiology. Zeke had been a star on the football team, quarterbacking Coastal Alabama to victory over their arch rival Alabama Auto Tech 24-17. After college Zeke was hired by the Department of Transportation to be a junior investigator in their Birmingham office. Zeke applied himself and after three years readied himself for promotion. It was no surprise that he was soon offered a job heading up the DOT office in Burnsville, Minnesota.

Although a culture and weather shock, Zeke soon settled into his new life as a Minnesotan. Twenty years seemed to have flown by and the work had grown somewhat routine. There were the usual road inspections, upgrade recommendations, the overseeing of construction projects, the removal of deer from someone's windshield, but nothing out of the ordinary – until that fateful evening.

Zeke pulled up to the accident scene which resembled more of an airplane crash than that of an automobile pile-up. Lights flashed from many directions from the many emergency vehicles that had assembled at the scene. As Zeke pulled over to the side of the road, he could see the carnage was immense. Never had he seen such devastation. Cars crumpled together in some Dali-esque junk yard – the only thing missing was a melted antique stopwatch draped over a nearby tree branch. Smoke engulfed the scene, making it difficult to see and breathe. Mangled metal was strewn for more than two hundred feet.

A shaken sergeant Larabie of the Highway patrol greeted Zeke as he emerged slowly from his truck. "Zeke, I'm glad Fargo got a hold of you. It's like a battlefield over here! You won't believe it!" said the shaken officer.

Sergeant Larabie escorted Zeke through the crash scene describing what the police felt had happened. From appearances, a man driving a silver BMW had merged into a single lane that had been occupied by a semi-trailer truck. The long, circular off-ramp leading from Highway 169 to Highway 101 starts off as a single lane. Those vehicles departing 169 take this single lane which curves from the south to the east. As the road curves, it joins the eastbound 101. For a stretch of a quarter of a mile the 169 off-ramp and a single lane of the 101 are parallel, gradually merging into one lane. It was here that the horrific accident occurred.

It appeared that the BMW had decided to merge late where the single lane began. The driver of the semi did not permit the driver of the BMW to merge. It was an unwritten law in Minnesota that immediately you know which lane you need to merge with, you promptly throw yourself into that lane at all costs. To delay your merge to within several yards of a single lane would be an outrage in Minnesota. It is something so vile that Minnesotans can barely bring themselves to talk about such an extreme. In their mind it is the ultimate in arrogance to merge at the last moment.

The problem was that the driver of the BMW was a fairly recent transplant from California. In California, merging is considered to be an art-form. Merging in California is like chess. You plan your attack, sizing up the cars in front of you and keeping an eye on the signs for your off-ramp. You calculate the distance to the off-ramp along with the speed of your car and those around you. You then estimate the number of cars in front. Based on the "openness" of other lanes you make your move. You accelerate and proceed to the next emptiest lane. As you proceed past slower cars you again calculate speed and distance. The fact that an off-ramp is less than a mile away is not cause for panic – stay in your lane, enjoy the physics! As the off-ramp comes closer, you gauge how many cars are in the farthest lane that you will eventually need to merge with. If there are too many cars you confidently look for openings. No openings? Still not time to panic. As a Californian you are the master of the rhythm and the beat of the California freeway system. You subconsciously know when you need to merge. At first it involves the conscious calculation of speed and the amount of cars to overtake, but eventually it is ingrained into your subconscious.

Sergeant Larabie continued his hypothesis, stating that the driver of the BMW had forced his way into the lane of the semi. Apparently the BMW squeezed in behind another car, but the infuriated truck driver must have accelerated, sandwiching the BMW between the truck and the car in front. What happened next was a chain reaction. The forces of the semi were so great that it sent the BMW smashing into the backend of the car in front of him, and in turn that car smashed into the car in front of it. This caused a chain reaction of these cars crashing into fifteen more cars in front of them.

All of the cars locked bumpers and began to barrel out of control like a runaway locomotive. The first car in line went careening off to the side of the road, bringing all of the other cars behind it into a large grassy knoll. It was there that the cars came into a pulverizing heap with the semi barreling into the back of them, causing a huge explosion. Four people were killed and the remaining twenty-three persons were in critical condition – none of them capable of confirming what had happened, and seven of them behind on their insurance premiums.

As sergeant Larabie finished his explanation, two men appeared out of the smoke and approached Zeke. Zeke quickly recognized one of the gentlemen as Hank Fargo, the police chief of Shakopee. The other gentleman was not familiar to him.

"Hey, Zeke!" shouted the chief.

"Hey, Chief!" Zeke shouted back.

"Looks like you've got quite a mess here!"

"I've never seen anything like this in my twenty-nine years of law enforcement. Zeke, I'd like you to meet Farrell Hardhart. He's our new psychiatrist."

"Hmmm, criminal psychiatrist, Mr. Hardhart?"

"No. Please call me Farrell. I'm a fully qualified post-trauma psychiatrist. I studied criminal psychiatry, but am on-board to lend a hand not only with criminals, but with counseling of patrol officers, family members, regular citizens, and to help people cope with major catastrophes like this one."

Zeke surveyed the good doctor's appearance, surmising his prep school looks had placed him at Harvard or some other Ivy League institution. He also pondered the need to have a police psychiatrist for a town of only 6,000 people. There typically were not too many maladjusted citizens in such a small, Midwest prairie town . . . with the exception of one lunatic farmer who began cryogenic experiments in an attempt to bring his dead cow back to life. His experiment went awry when he left the lid off the cryogenic tank and several other creatures, including his mother-in-law, accidentally stumbled in. In any event, Zeke was not paid to ponder.

"Zeke, I'd like you to get to know Farrell. He has a lot to share with you about this case. I think what information he has will be of great interest to you."

"Investigator Martin, do you think we can grab some coffee somewhere?"

"Sure, and please call me Zeke. Yah, why don't we head into Shakopee? I'll meet you at Froggy's Bar. Know the place?"

"Know it! I practically live there. Wings night on Thursdays with $1.50 Buds. Great flat-screen TV to catch the Huskers on Saturdays. I can't tell you the number of times I had to call my wife to come pick me up."

Zeke looked at Dr. Hardhart with a stunned look on his face. The preppy doctor sounded like one of the pool hall rats that hung out at Froggy's on a regular basis. Maybe he would like this guy after all.

After a quick ten minute drive into downtown Shakopee, both men pulled into Froggy's. Dr. Hardhart quickly ushered Zeke through the entrance and requested a booth for two. The two men made small talk while an elderly waitress approached them with the apparent intention of asking for their order.

"Yes, I'll have a slab of blueberry pie with some coffee – black," cried the plucky young doctor.

"Ditto for me, Madge!"

Before the men could return to their conversation, they noticed Madge had fallen asleep halfway through the order.

"Madge . . . Madge!"

Zeke's voice awoke the startled server. Madge Wilson was ninety-seven years old and was a Shakopee celebrity. She once appeared on the David Letterman show two years ago. The then ninety-five year old was famous for never having ever stepped foot out of Shakopee. She had never gone to nearby Bloomington, home to the Mall of Minnesota, or neighboring Burnsville. Her only cross-border excursion was in 1973 for a doctor's visit in Savage, the city to the east of Shakopee.

Her appearance on the David Letterman Show degenerated into a confused conversation where the host admonished Madge for her lack of travel, but Madge continuing to state that she had in fact traveled by virtue of her coming to New York to do the show – this to her invalidated the necessity for her appearance. Letterman just smiled and nodded, all the while planning the fate of the producer who had scheduled the show.

Once Madge had been fully awoken and sent on her way,

the men continued their conversation. After musing over Madge's history, Dr. Hardhart soon turned serious. He opened his briefcase and produced a notebook and a CD. Before Dr. Hardhart could explain about the CD, a young man burst into the front entrance, quickly spotted Zeke and ran over to him.

"Jimmy, what's the matter?" Zeke asked, with a strained look on his face.

"Oh nothing. I just like quickly intruding on people's conversations with a panicked look on my face!"

"Oh . . . okay. Dr. Hardhart, I'd like you to meet my assistant Jimmy Tinzdale."

"Hi, Jimmy, how are you?"

"Great, if you like chaos and tragedy."

"Hmmm, you mean that crash over on the 169?"

"No, I mean my wife is making me salad again for dinner. Have you heard of such a thing? I mean, salad for dinner? I'm a man. I need protein and nutrition."

Jimmy Tinzdale was Zeke's right-hand, although Zeke would probably prefer he be his left-foot – the one with the corn on it. Jimmy was a fireplug. Nothing fazed him at all. He had been a football and track star in high school and was probably on his way to the pros as an offensive lineman until that fateful game – November 16th, 1990. The game was Burnsville high school versus Prior Lake. Jimmy was going deep for a pass, which was unusual. As previously mentioned, he was a lineman. He went headlong into the goal post and completely knocked it over. He never seemed the same after that.

He later went on to college but could never play football

again. Instead, he went into radiology but later had to quit because there were problems with the metal plate in his head. Like Zeke's dad, Jimmy was adding to the growing population of metal plate-headed citizens in the southern suburbs.

It was DOT director Harry Waxhead, Jimmy's uncle who later got him a place in Zeke's office as his assistant. There was no government grade for such a position. Technically Malaysia St. Croix filled that position and filled it nicely – but Waxhead could pull strings, and strings he thus pulled.

"Ah, is there anything I can do for you, Jimmy?"

"Yah, you called me over here to help you."

"No I didn't."

"Yes, you did."

"No I didn't"

"Yes, you did."

This pointless bickering continued for several minutes when Zeke finally tired.

"Okay, if I called you let me see your cell – it should have all of your inbound calls correct?"

Jimmy became silent. "It's that damn parrot again that my wife bought for the kids."

Both Hardhart and Zeke shook their heads in confusion.

"There's a problem with the parrot?" Zeke said, still completely baffled by any connection to a previous phone call.

"Yah, it's my wife. She's trained that parrot to sound like you, Zeke. The damn thing can even sound like the ring tones I select."

Zeke took a long hard stare at Jimmy and began

dreaming of some far off land that he could ban him to.

"Well, Jimmy, you can do one of two things. You can head home to your salad, or go out and find a dog to replace your parrot – it's entirely up to you."

Zeke had given in to Waxhead regarding Jimmy and was not the type to push the higher powers. If Waxhead wanted Jimmy in his office, then there Jimmy would stay. As long as he didn't interfere with Zeke's work he didn't care if Jimmy was selling arms to North Korea in the back room.

With a rather perturbed look on his face, Jimmy gathered his baseball cap and proceeded out the front door. He sped off in a huff, which was too bad since he drove a Buick.

"Zeke, you are never going to believe what is on this CD, or what's in this notebook."

Zeke was silent, but riveted by Hardhart's display.

"This CD and notebook contain the diaries and reports from a young man by the name of Trent Mallard."

"Like the duck?"

"Like the duck."

Dr. Hardhart stared at Zeke as though the young man's name should have some sort of significance for him. Zeke silently shook his head indicating he was unsure who Mr. Mallard was. Hardhart went on to explain that Trent Mallard was a recent transplant from California, having arrived within the past four months. Mallard had just started with McKenzie, Laughlin, McAllister, Wiggenbothom, Samstrung, Filibuster and Associates as an architect, having just graduating from the University of Southern California.

After arriving in Minnesota, Mallard had difficulty not only adapting to the weather and change in culture, but with the highway system and driving technique of Minnesota. Mallard had often been found quarreling with his fellow co-workers over what he deemed as their peculiar driving styles and the "terrible way in which the highway system had been laid out." He would regale his colleagues on the efficient and intricate workings of the Los Angeles freeway system, and would compare Minnesota streets and highways as "inferior to even the back-roads and trails found in Bulgaria."

"How do you know all this?" queried Zeke, noting that the accident had happened within the past two hours.

"Well, Mallard had been so fed-up with the driving in Minnesota that he contacted the Sheriff within two weeks of his arrival her to complain about the streets. Plus, we wanted the plot to move along more quickly."

"Oh, I see." Zeke nodded, completely confused by the last comment.

"Why did he contact the Sheriff here in Shakopee? Did he live here?"

"Yah, just off of Marshall, over by the new town-homes they're building by the hospital."

"Poor sap," Zeke sighed to himself.

"Imagine moving from Los Angeles, California to Shakopee, Minnesota."

Both men shook their heads in utter amazement and compassion for the deceased Angelean.

"Pheww, that would be like putting a race horse in a merry-go-round."

Dr. Hardhart smiled and nodded politely, having no idea

what in the world Zeke meant by that analogy.

For the next several hours both men poured over Mallard's diary and listened to the CD he recorded from his car. Dr. Hardhart explained that Mallard had become so frustrated with the driving in Minnesota that not only did he create a journal of incidents, but kept a voice recorder with him in his car using it as a type of black box to capture his comments, and to be able to explain what might have happened in the case of an accident.

As the men delved through the myriad of editorials and descriptions Mallard had put together, it soon became evident that the main problem that Mallard had experienced was merging in Minnesota.

After years of fluid maneuvering and merging on the streets and freeways of LA, Mallard described his situation as "descending into traffic flow hell!" "This was Dante's true vision of the chaos and torture of the *Inferno*," Mallard muttered to himself on one part of the CD, adding that the freeways of Minnesota were a "perpetual roadblock."

"No one in this state truly understands the concept of merging!" wrote a tortured Mallard on December 17th.

"As soon as they enter the on-ramp they look for an immediate opening in the traffic, and in a panicked flurry throw themselves into that opening with no regard to the speed of the person they are merging in front of. And if there is no opening, they prefer to sit in the on-ramp, waiting for an opening – this is because the average driver here in Minnesota would prefer to force that poor driver to sit there in a potentially dangerous situation and not let the person merge in front of them – there is no fluidity. No rhythm.

Minnesotans pay dearly for their bit of highway they are driving on, and you had better not merge in front of them. I can't recall the number of times I have indicated I wanted to make a lane change, only to find that the driver behind me had accelerated in order that I cannot enter that lane. It's like a large racing flag is waved every time I flip on the blinker to make a lane change – what's with these people? Merging is an art, and clearly Minnesotans are not art-lovers."

Dr. Hardhart and Zeke continued to digest the contents of Mallard's journal, accepting occasional offers from Marge to refill their depleted coffee cups.

"Look at this, Zeke." He passed over the notebook.

"The other morning I needed to drive over to Eagan to pick up some drafting materials. I allotted a reasonable amount of time to depart Shakopee, go to Eagan, and then to drive back to work in Eden Prairie. As I arrived into Eagan from Burnsville on the 35 East freeway, I encountered a huge queue of cars in the right-hand lane. This line-up must have been two miles long prior to my exit on the 494 freeway. 'What could be the cause of this congestion? I pondered to myself, and then proceeded onward in the far left-hand lane.

"Traffic was moving smoothly in the two outside lanes, but as I continued toward the 494 I noticed traffic in the right-hand lane was at a virtual standstill. 'They must be exiting on a nearby off-ramp,' I concluded, and again continued toward the 494. It was then that I slowly realized to my horror that this queue of cars was waiting to get off on the 494.

"I now noticed that a mile beyond where the initial queue had began, there were cars frantically trying to merge – drivers with panicked looks in their faces chaotically hurtling themselves into the right-hand lane. They were like lemmings throwing themselves off cliffs, or in this case into the right-hand lane with little regard for the space, speed and distance of the nearest car. Surely these were newcomers to Eagan, realizing late that their off-ramp was fast approaching? But I realized, no. These were drivers merging two miles, TWO MILES before their exit on to 494.

"'Do these people understand the concept of merging?' I screamed silently to myself in anguish, knowing that had I been in LA there would be no queue, no chaotic scrambling to get over to the right-hand lane. Just easy maneuvering with the intent of eventually moving into the right-hand lane some one hundred yards prior to the off-ramp. And why were these people so crazed to merge prematurely? Because they knew their fellow Minnesotans would not permit them to merge closer to the off-ramp. To merge late was arrogance on your part. To make a smooth transition within a short distance of your exit was intolerable. You must merge miles prior to your exit. You must plan ahead and not be caught with a last moment departure from the freeway. This is the unwritten Minnesota law."

Hardhart and Zeke went on to read how Mallard had battled with the same early merging syndrome on the on-ramp that led from the highway 101 to the highway 169 in Savage on his way to work every morning. As he would try and drive onto the northbound 169, cars would be trying to fling themselves in front of him, hoping to give themselves plenty of time to exit off of the Old Shakopee Road exit, which was a mile further down.

Mallard had grown so obsessed with the "Early Merging Syndrome" that he had started to write down descriptions of drivers and their cars, as well as license plates of those who perpetually merged early. His hope was one day being able to call these people and instruct them on the art of merging.

Clearly Mallard was a troubled man – to Dr. Hardhart anyway. For Zeke, he understood. Being a transplant he had also fought the battles of Mallard, but being the even-tempered Southerner he was, he had continually let it go by him. But now he had seen this phenomenon come to its ultimate conclusion and he understood clearly why it had happened.

As the two men realized it was past midnight, and that their spouses would be concerned, they decided to bid Marge adieu and head home. They both made plans to meet in Dr. Hardhart's office the following Monday morning, and then departed the cafe.

CHAPTER 2

The next morning Zeke awoke to the phone blaring in his ear. It was Steve Barnhead from the Star Tribune.

"Zeke! What are your thoughts about the accident? Or the Savagery in Savage? Or the South Metro Mayhem? . . . How 'bout the Shocker in Shakopee? Good headlines, eh?"

In his R.E.M.-deprived haze, Zeke replied as best as he could. "Who are you?!!!" he yelled into the phone.

After explaining who he was, Barnhead again asked for Zeke's comments on the accident. Zeke replied unintelligibly.

Barnhead then asked Zeke what he thought about the four deaths involved in the accident. Zeke, when remembering four people had been killed, suddenly snapped into a state of complete consciousness.

"Well . . . "

Zeke had not fully digested the full details of the accident; four dead, including Mallard, three in critical condition, ten in stable condition and eight more in intensive care. It seemed to Zeke that merging in Minnesota had become a deadly game.

"Well, Zeke, what do you think?" the reporter persisted.

"Well, it's a tragedy, that's what I think."

"What will be your next move?"

"I plan to have a shower and a shave."

"No, I mean with regard to the accident."

"We will launch a thorough investigation into the cause of the accident, as we always do."

Zeke waited for a response or another question from the feisty reporter.

"Sorry, Zeke, I didn't quite catch that. I'm on my cell phone and I think I'm out of coverage. You said something about 'you always do . . . '? Do what?"

"We always do investigations into the cause of accidents."

Again there was complete silence on the other end of the line.

"You said something about your investigations cause accidents – why would that be?" The reporter's voice was breaking up.

Zeke stared up to the ceiling wondering why this babbling reporter was bothering him. "No, that's not what I said. Whenever there are accidents we do a thorough and exhaustive investigation."

Zeke could hear some crackling on the other end of the line and again wondered if the reporter had heard what he had said. He could hear the reporter's voice coming in and out.

"Okay, let me see if I have this straight. Your exhausted, and sometimes when investigating it leads to more accidents. Did I get that right?"

Zeke launched into a tirade of expletives and insults that would have made a conman blush – assuming conmen can blush.

"Alright, Zeke, I'll make sure this gets published right away. Anything else you'd like to add?"

Again Zeke screamed and yelled into the phone, trying to somehow communicate to the incoherent reporter.

"Zeke, can't quite hear you, but I appreciate your time."

Besides going to St. John the Baptist for Sunday Mass, Zeke spent the remainder of the weekend going over Mallard's journal. It was like going over the diary of a war correspondent during the Vietnam War, with the only thing missing being napalm.

Mallard had painted a clear picture that it was he alone with a few "outsiders" against the world, or in this case, Minnesota drivers. He would meticulously detail each incident – giving in-depth commentary as to what a driver should and should not have done in a particular situation. What struck Zeke the most was the obsession the man had with Minnesotans' lack of merging etiquette and technique. He surmised this was probably a person who would not have given merging a second thought in his native California.

Zeke read another excerpt from Mallard's diary:

"It was a day like any other day in Minnesota, a day to strap on the racing helmet and get ready for whatever lay ahead. I departed my townhouse at 8:15 am and proceeded to Highway 13. Avoiding the long line of lemmings on Highway 101, I proceeded into the left lane until I was within a quarter of a mile of the 101 West off-ramp which changes into the 169 North on-ramp. I saw a relatively wide gap in front of a '99 Dodge Neon and proceeded to merge. I could see the line in front of the Neon starting to simultaneously brake as usual, probably the result of the mass merging of cars at the head of the on-ramp of 169 North. Seeing the cars braking, I adeptly slipped into the gap, having slowed to meet the speed of the cars preceding the Neon.

"Several cars in the left lane from whence I had came, proceeded to pummel me with shouts and honking of their horns in disapproval that I had left it so late to merge, and for having them slow by 0.0016 percent of the speed they had previously had been roaring along at. The inconvenience must have been a considerable hardship for these men and women of the North. As I proceeded on the on-ramp, I braced myself for the impending mass migration of cars that were coming north from Shakopee on 169, and who were wanting to merge with the far right lane (the same lane the 101 East folks were merging into) to get over to the Old Shakopee Road off-ramp. The unfortunate thing was the Old Shakopee Road was one mile from where the 101 East joined 169 North, and it was entirely unnecessary to be merging that prematurely.

"In any event, I knew what I was up against. Would it be the surly executive bent on giving no ground within the confines of his lane? Or would it be the snooty old receptionist, who from a lack of a decent career decides to take it out on her fellow commuters? Perhaps it would be the militant union rep from some factory, who would live by the book when it came to the factory union rules but ignore others if he became inconvenienced. Maybe it was the deer hunter who at times couldn't distinguish between what was wildlife and human. Surprisingly it was the grocery truck driver who flung himself in front of me first.

"As I allowed the truck to merge in front of me, I could then see a Ford Windstar pull into the lane where the grocery truck had just been. The mini-van was parallel to my front bumper and to the back bumper of the grocery truck. The driver was frantically signaling; flipping her head back and forth to see if a large enough gap was appearing between me and the grocery truck. I could see the poor woman's concern slowly turning to panic. The woman in her early thirties was probably a very successful professional, with a family – several car seats were strapped into the back, but thankfully they were empty. Had her children been attached they probably would have been suffering from whiplash by now, given her constant accelerating and then suddenly stopping.

"For me it had become a game. The woman could easily accelerate and merge a bit farther down the road in front of the grocery truck – and yet, like many of her fellow Minnesotans, she must merge and merge at the earliest moment possible.

"I smiled with a very bemused expression as I studied the poor woman's moves. She kept looking at me with a type of look that indicated she wanted me to either completely stop, or accelerate like some start to a NASCAR race. But no, it was my moral duty to set this poor, lost soul straight.

"'Maintain a constant speed. The art in merging lies in keeping a constant speed and then wait for an opening. If an opening doesn't appear, then calmly slow your vehicle or accelerate your vehicle to another part of the lane you wish to merge with.' The woman again looked to me with a look of consternation that said, 'Why can't you move?' I could see her silently scream from her car.

"Now the woman was starting to weave. She could not comprehend why the driver parallel to her was not stopping for her. It did not occur to her to accelerate to another ten to fifteen miles above her current speed to bypass myself and the grocery truck and merge gracefully and confidently into the wide-open lane that lay ahead of the grocery truck. But she did not have the forward vision of a Southern California driver. But she could also simply slow down and slip in behind me. It was simple – but not so simple for the driver of the Northern Plains.

"Eventually she decided to accelerate into the gap in front of me. The lane had slowed to a speed of thirty-five miles an hour. I usually left a gap that represented a car length for every ten miles an hour of speed. The problem was, as soon as she finally made her decision to merge, the grocery truck had to brake for a fast moving SUV that decided to suddenly, and without warning, throw itself into the lane in front of the grocery truck.

With the gap between me and the grocery truck slowly dissipating, the Windstar came barreling into the gap in front of me, and smashed into the back of the grocery truck. I instinctively and adeptly swerved into the shoulder, squeezed around the two entangled vehicles and slipped in right behind the SUV. As I continued on, I could see in the rearview mirror the man in the grocery truck getting out of his cab and make his way toward the Windstar. As they faded from view, I could see the two poor drivers exchanging information. Another smooth commute to work. Where else could I find so much excitement?"

Zeke noted Mallard's sarcastic salutation and sighed to himself as he sensed the tremendous frustration that must have been building in the young architect.

For the next week, Zeke poured over Mallard's recordings and diaries. In a search of Mallard's condo, three more diaries were discovered. Again, as his previous writings indicated, he was the tortured soul of a young Californian trying to make his way in the Midwest. Zeke could see that Mallard's obsession had grown to the point that he was even conducting experiments and making reports.

On his regular commute up the 169 each morning, he decided to start identifying cars. In a separate journal he would write down the make and model of the cars, their license plate numbers and a brief description of the drivers. He even gave some of the drivers names like, "Farmer Brown," "Ice-Lady," "Spaz-Man," and "Panicky Pam." One of Mallard's funniest quips was that Minnesota was the Land of 10,000 passive aggressives."

One study Mallard made was when and where various drivers merged. He often was frustrated when someone would start signaling to merge in front of him, when clearly there was no room to merge. On several occasions he could see that there was a crossroad approaching and thus assumed that the driver intending to merge wanted to get into the left-hand turn lane in order to turn left at the oncoming crossroad. Noting their desire to want to turn left, Mallard graciously would slow down to allow them to turn left. However on many of the occasions the driver, rather than turning left, would continue on through the intersection.

They then would turn at a following intersection sometimes a mile beyond. This again, in Mallard's opinion, was premature merging which severely impeded the natural flow of traffic. If Minnesotans would simply merge closer to their turns or exits within one hundred yards, all of this congestion and swerving and near misses could be avoided.

It was clear to Zeke that Mallard was awake at night, obsessed with how Minnesotans drive, and making it his mission to see that they came to be aware of the errors of their ways.

Zeke, to his own surprise, began to have sympathy for the young rebel. He too had endured the strange driving habits of the native Minnesotans. Being a highway inspector, he had enjoyed traveling the roads of almost every state in the nation. He had always been impressed with the LA freeway system – a system that allowed for the easy flow of traffic. It was a system with plenty of access as well as ability to frequently depart at almost any major side street. The on/off-ramps were a joy. Usually very long, the ramps would allow its users plenty of time to enter or exit. As Zeke discovered, one of Mallard's main contentions was the antiquated highway system of the Twin Cities.

"Clearly this is a system developed in the 1950s, with little attention paid to it since its inception," lamented a frustrated Mallard.

Zeke had shared the same frustrations as Mallard, often complaining to MNDOT for more planning when it came to expansion and updating of the current road structure. Due to the severe Minnesota winters and the beatings the highways took, it would be difficult enough just to keep the current roads up, let alone trying to modernize the overall system.

Despite this, Zeke had implore MNDOT officials to meet with CalTrans officials from California to discuss flow strategies, but MNDOT would push back claiming that CalTrans personnel could not understand the culture of Minnesota. He did not give up though and would continually call Peter Wetmarsh at the MNDOT main office to complain about the conditions of the roads.

Zeke's own frustration with Minnesota drivers and his lack of getting anywhere with MNDOT prompted him to call Director Waxhead. Zeke's relationship with Waxhead was cordial but at times contentious. Zeke took pride in his work and looked at the smallest of details which Waxhead didn't have time for. This irritated Waxhead, and often put the two at odds with each other.

"Director Waxhead, Zeke Martin here."

"Yes, Zeke, what can I do you for," came Waxhead's contentious and blustery response.

"Director, I have been pouring over the diaries and recordings of that poor soul Mallard who was involved in the pile up the other day. This man made some rather detailed studies that I think we need to pay attention to . . ."

"Studies . . . what kind of studies?"

"Well, he would study the trends and techniques that

Minnesota drivers have when it comes to merging. I think a lot of what he discovered is worthwhile for us to look at."

"Now, Zeke, let's not jump to any conclusions here. I mean we are not Californians, remember? You probably think of us as country bumpkins on our way for a Sunday drive, but we have a system in place and it works."

Zeke rolled his eyes. This was the 11,567th time he had heard those words – "We have a system in place and it works." Zeke felt to the contrary.

"Yes, Director, but this also confirms some unofficial studies and observations I have made as well."

"Studies? What studies? I don't pay you to make studies, Martin. I pay you to go out and clean things up."

"Hmmm, that's not what my job description said when I signed on here. I am to do analysis of the roads and to help prevent accidents."

"You are? Who is this again?"

"Zeke Martin, Director."

"Oh, Martin. I thought you said Martini."

"Martini? We have a Martini in the department?"

"No, but I'd like one. Anyway, Martin, I think we have a system in place and I think it works quite nicely. Now good day to you, sir."

With that Waxhead hung up the phone. Zeke looked out the window toward the horizon wondering how he ever got himself into this department. Zeke pondered for awhile watching Malaysia work frantically on a spreadsheet that he needed help with.

Zeke admired Malaysia. God was working overtime when he created her. He kept this thought to himself. He could easily get distracted when watching her. He often thought what things would have been like had he met her when he was young and single. Zeke grew up in the south in the Bible-belt. He had always gone to church, believed in God and the thought of an extra-marital affair was conflicting with his nature to say the least. Zeke had been tempted before but not like this. "God, why do you tempt us men so?" he screamed silently. He began looking around the office, realizing he hadn't screamed silently.

"Something wrong, Zeke?" Bill Felt, the assistant dispatcher asked.

"No, I'm fine."

Malaysia was just too gosh darn beautiful. She often wore form-fitting dresses that appeared to be almost like silk. They had an Asian look to them with floral patterns that made him dream of them both frolicking on some beach in Polynesia. Her femininity was a frustration to him – it seemed to overpower everything and everyone around her. Malaysia would of course act innocent of wielding such power. She was a goddess to him.

"Say, Bill, could you get a hold of Fred Dander from the Multi-media department and have him meet me over at the 169 – The Bloomington Ferry Bridge near highway 101? Tell him to bring all of his fancy video stuff as well."

It was all Zeke could do to get himself out of the office. Malaysia was becoming too hard to deal with. But that was his problem, he thought to himself. He shouldn't let his feelings impact her career. He would have to do something to take his mind off of her and do it quick. The 169 accident was probably the only thing that was going to do that.

Malaysia St. Croix was an enigma to Zeke. She was a beautiful, bubbly blonde who at times could be quite witty and intelligent, and at other times quite ditzy.

She received her name from the country of her conception – her parents honeymooned in Kuala Lumpur. She, however, bore little resemblance to the Malay people. She was a cross between Marilyn Monroe and Madonna, although both of those stars pretty much resemble the same person, whoever that is.

Malaysia graduated from MIT with a degree in Astro-Physics, which made Zeke wonder why in the world she was an administrative assistant for the Department of Transportation in Burnsville, Minnesota. From the bits and pieces he had heard there were apparently some issues during her days at NASA. Something about leaving a screwdriver in one of the rocket intake valves, and another story about uploading personal MapQuest results into the guidance system of the shuttle. In any event, she retained her government pay grade level but was re-assigned to a completely different agency.

Malaysia was invaluable to Zeke. She was on top of everything and at times a step ahead of him. Although he appreciated her work, he was frustrated that with all of her education she could be wasting it as an admin. On the other hand she could be ditzy. Her NASA problems seemed at times to trail her to the Department of Transportation. She had accidentally set Zeke's desk ablaze with a coffee maker that she had re-wired incorrectly, had driven her car through a restaurant drive-through (literally), and had created a fifteen car pile-up in Burnsville – which later Zeke had to investigate. It was quite an embarrassment to the department, but Zeke smoothed it over as best as he could.

The bottom line was Zeke loved Malaysia. Not so much in the romantic way, but more because of her humanness. She was herself. Sure she could be clumsy and ditzy, but she was also a lot of fun, pretty and smart. There were many a Friday when things were winding down that Malaysia would pop on one of her favorite CDs and force Zeke to dance around the office with her. Zeke loved her spontaneity and couldn't resist doing the Hokey Pokey with her or the Macarena, or the Stairway to Heaven – the latter would look pretty weird.

Beyond everything else, the most important thing for Zeke was Malaysia was a good sounding board. The other investigators in the office were off on their own assignments, each looking for a case that would make them stand-out and get them a quick promotion. Tagging along with Zeke was not going to get them any acclaim, and that was fine as far as Zeke was concerned – he liked to delegate, not micromanage his staff. All Zeke needed was a flashlight, his truck, and a good discussion with Malaysia to figure out the latest accident or to put together a good proposal for street renovations.

Zeke decided to talk to Malaysia about the Shakopee disaster to get her input.

"Malaysia," he muttered, as he tried to sip his coffee and speak at the same time.

"Are you talking to me, Zeke?" Malaysia questioned, as she swayed to the sounds of the latest heavy metal hit from the radio.

"Malaysia, what is that you're listening to on the radio?"

"Oh it's the latest hit from Heavy Robot Death Torture. It's called *Sunday Picnic*."

Instead of getting Malaysia's input, Zeke decided to just go ahead with his idea of a traffic video study.

Some twenty minutes later he met up with Fred Dander from Multi-media. There was always a type of unspoken tension between the rest of the department and the multi-media geeks. The problem was that neither spoke the other's language. The investigators knew nothing about movie and film production or anything too technology oriented – likewise the multi-media guys knew nothing of the ins-and-outs of highway investigating. For the most part Zeke and Dander got along, but it could be hard for Zeke to communicate what he wanted.

"Hey, Martin, are we ready to shoot this thing?" Dander came over to Zeke near where he had parked on the side of the interstate. Dander was wearing a French beret and was smoking a cigarette on a long cigarette holder, constantly tipping ashes on to Zeke's boots. Zeke had a double-take as Dander looked like a director from some 1930s movie set. He had an assistant with him that was carrying a couple of boxes that appeared to contain movie equipment.

Fred Dander had been a film major at the University of Wisconsin. He made his own films in his spare time, but had been frustrated at not getting any distribution deals or any local theaters to take his films. Apart from the three hundred and eleven porn films he had made, he described himself as a Avant Guard film maker.

His senior film at the U of W was entitled "Two Men,

Two Women and a Box of Kleenex." Primarily shot around the city of Madison, it centered on the exploits of four college students trying to buy Kleenex in the middle of the night. Shot entirely in black and white with often cloudy images, Dander claimed he was trying to capture "humanity in its ultimate frustration." The movie ends in a shoot-out with the four students being killed by police while trying to hold up a convenience store.

"Okay, Zeke, what are we going for here? A documentary on the plight of the everyday American worker? A cinematic spectacle on the modern machine – man versus machine?"

"No, I just want you to attach the camera to the light pole and film traffic for the entire month starting now. Got it?"

Dander looked sheepish. This is not what he had dreamed of when he had signed on as the head of the multimedia group for the Department of Transportation. His assistant, barely able to see through the hair in his eyes, just stared at Dander while waiting for further instructions.

"This is what you dragged me out here for, Martin? Don't you have any appreciation for the artist?"

"No, now get to work . . . and I want that film put together pronto! Oh, and I'll want an updated tape each week sent to my office."

As Zeke bid farewell to Dander, Jimmy Tinzdale came zooming up in a cloud of dust and dirt in his new gold-colored Crown Victoria that had "Minnesota State Transportation Department" plastered all over it. Zeke resented the fact that Jimmy could be allocated such a nice car and be a junior assistant in the office – once again the perks of being Waxhead's nephew.

"Okay, Zeke, what's going on here?" Jimmy practically screamed, as he slammed the door.

"Whoa, Jimmy, slow down there – we might have to get you a squad car if you keep burnin' down the highway like that."

"Never mind that. What's going on?"

"What's going on is none of your business."

"Everything's my business, Zeke, Uncle . . . I mean Harry Waxhead has given me responsibility for the office budget this year. I need to watch every penny carefully."

Zeke shook his head in contempt for the overzealous junior assistant.

"So what have we here?" Jimmy said, like some sadistic Gestapo officer.

"This is Fred Dander from the multi-media department. He's helping me with a little study."

"Study, eh? Study of what?"

"Well, we're showing a high number of accidents occurring in this area, and we'd like to do a time-study."

"I see," Jimmy said, as he walked around the camera, hands behind his back acting like a hardened interrogator.

"You know, Zeke, in Alabama you might have some fancy movie equipment to study time, but here in Minnesota we do things differently. Here in Minnesota we are more practical than those fancy-pants investigators down in Birmingham or Huntstown . . ."

"Huntsville."

"Whatever. Anyway, here in Minnesota we take a different approach. The bottom-line is accidents are going to happen. It's a fact of life. It's like what Jesus said, 'the poor you will have with you always.'"

Zeke and Dander starred at each other in amazement, wondering what Jimmy was raving about, and the fact that he could make a Biblical reference.

"And what do you mean by that comment?"

"Well, like the poor, we will always have accidents – they're inevitable."

"So we just give up?"

"No, of course not. You know . . . you do charity work occasionally which will ease your conscience, and by doing so you think you're helping the poor, which, in reality like Jesus said, it's not really doing anything because they'll always be around, but you do your best and you move on. Likewise, you keep your eye on traffic and do the best you can. Right, Fred?"

"Right," Fred said, without knowing what Jimmy was talking about.

"So what do you think, F-R-E-D?" Jimmy said, with emphasis on the letters, leading him to try and make some sort of conclusion. Fred looked at Jimmy with pursed lips, shaking his head and then trying to mouth words that might make Jimmy leave him alone.

"I think we will make . . . ," he said, looking for Jimmy's approval.

"A movie about poor people's driving habits in Minnesota!" Fred shrieked, thinking he had concluded correctly.

Jimmy slapped his hand on his forehead and started to mutter something that sounded like a cross between Gaelic and Arabic.

"Look, Jimmy, the bottom-line here is I am the boss. I don't care what the budget says. We need to do a time-study, not a study of time – a time-study that covers a month period so we can study the average amount of accidents that occur in this area. If you have a problem with it, then take it up with your uncle."

With that Zeke got into his car and headed back to the office. Things were getting weird these days in the streets and highways of Minnesota, and Zeke was bound and determined to figure out what was going on. He had always had a sneaking suspicion that there was something wrong with the way Minnesotans drove, and he was going to find out what it was.

Back at the office, Malaysia greeted him with a sandwich and a cup of coffee. Zeke immediately went to the Department of Motor Vehicle files and pulled out a copy of the latest driving test. He scoured it from top to bottom, looking over each question:

Question 21:

When maintaining a safe distance between yourself and the car in front of you, what is a good rule of thumb to remember?

A) Pretend there is an imaginary measuring tape stretched out in front of you.

B) Keep a car length distance for every 10 miles an hour you are driving.

C) Keep 50 feet behind the car in front of you.

D) Accelerate and brake incessantly to hopefully avoid accidents.

It was question 22 that threw him . . .

Question 22*:
Give the procedure for merging carefully.
A) *Move turn signal for the lane in which you are moving into. Turn to look behind you to see if there is any traffic. Slowly move into the lane you are merging into.*
B) *Move turn signal for the heck of it and head into the next lane without looking.*
C) *Accelerate car 10 miles an hour faster than you are currently going and force your way into the next lane.*
D) *Decelerate your car 20 miles an hour slower than you are currently going and force your way into the next lane.*
    *This question does not apply to residents of Minnesota

For Zeke, things were starting to make sense as to why people drove the way they did in Minnesota. He next pulled up a report he was working on in his computer. He had been monitoring various construction and upgrade projects within the highway and freeway system of the state. Part of the problem people had with merging in Minnesota was that not only did they appear to not understand how to merge, but the roads were set up in such a way as to make it difficult if not impossible to merge.

On some freeways the off-ramps and on-ramps were so

short that they were disasters waiting to happen. Zeke had been monitoring how projects were going as well as how many accidents were occurring at some of the suspect intersections.

CHAPTER 3

The following day, Zeke had Gloria take him to the airport. Zeke was to fly to Dallas for a two day seminar on new gravel and cement technologies. Before getting on the plane the two had lunch together at a nearby restaurant – Château LeBec. Zeke hated the place, but felt he needed to give Gloria a nice lunch somewhere. The Hamburger Helper was starting to go downhill in quality and he felt Gloria probably needed a break to refresh her self.

"Oh, Zeke, this is so wonderful. Thank you for taking me here." Gloria marveled at the décor in the entryway to the restaurant. It was a combination Greco-Chinese style which was interesting given that it was a French Restaurant.

"Bon jour, Monsewer. Duiex tablas por nos," Zeke said in something that was not French.

"Right this way," the dazed waiter motioned.

The restaurant was dark and if there was anything that Zeke Martin did not trust it was a dark restaurant. He wanted to see his food – he didn't want to guess what it was, or if someone had put something on it like ants or snails or something he thought the French might eat.

"Bon jour, polle vu francais?" the waiter, said with a snooty voice.

"We, keske vu preneg y illsont de bon bon?"

The waiter nodded his head, completely at a loss as to what Zeke was saying.

"May I explain to you the specials of the day?"

"We, we, mon ami."

"We have a pleasant trout almandine with asparagus and au gratin potatoes. The catch of the day is Tilapia, and the soup of the day is broccoli and cheese."

Zeke stared at the waiter dumbfounded, trying to understand how a fish from the Atlantic could be fresh. After shaking his head he ordered a hamburger and fries, and Gloria took the fondue.

"So, Zeke, how's the case been going?"

Zeke smiled at Gloria. She had been his first love. They met at one of his football games in college. He threw a last second touchdown against the Institute of Freeway Sciences in the first ever "McMillan Toll Way Bowl" held in Pensacola Florida. Gloria was a cheerleader, and when she saw Zeke throw that pass she wanted him to throw a pass at her. Unfortunately he did, and she got a bruise on her thigh.

Once graduated from college, he with a major in Highway Management and her in Mechanical Manuals Management with a minor in philosophy, they became engaged and married after Zeke was hired by the Alabama Department of Roads and Alleyways. They had three beautiful children, Mark, Felipe and Desiree. Gloria had always been a homemaker and she preferred it that way. She wanted to make sure the kids were looked after, and that was fine by Zeke. He enjoyed the home life and he loved his family.

Once the kids had grown and moved away, the relationship seemed to lose its luster. It was nothing intentional by either party, it was just routines they had grown accustomed to. Gloria would go out with her friends to clubs, or espresso bars to discuss Kant and Kierkegaard with local philosophers, while Zeke would go to a local bar or pub to commiserate with his friends. Zeke continued his love of sports, and would coach his sons' football and soccer teams, and his daughter's basketball teams. Once the children had left, he continued to be a coach to help out the local kids. Even when they moved to Minnesota he continued to coach sports. Both had their own lives and it was getting harder and harder to connect.

The one thing that seemed to always bring them together however was their physical attraction for each other. Although the frequency of their love-making had declined over the years, they still truly loved each other and tried to make each other happy. Zeke had fallen in love with a sleek, beautiful brunette, but the years were starting to show on Gloria. Three children had left her shape slightly flabby in places, but he understood that. He wasn't looking to replace Gloria, but he couldn't get Malaysia off his mind.

"So are you going to stare at me for fifteen minutes, or are you going to answer my question?"

"Oops, sorry! Ah, the case . . . the case is going okay. I'm not sure where it's going to lead, but I think it may be one of the most interesting I've had in quite a while."

"Why do you say that?"

"Well, I think we may confirm many suspicions I've had about Minnesota driving for quite some time. What's new with you?"

"Well, after I drop you off, the girls and I are going to Cirque du Soleil"

"Fantastic!" Zeke said having no clue what Cirque du Soleil was.

As their food arrived, Zeke quietly played with his food and admired Gloria. She had been a good wife. She had been faithful (he assumed), always tried to meet his needs physically and emotionally, and despite some twenty-five years of marriage, she was still attractive. So what that she had a flabby stomach – he would have a flabby stomach too if he had three seven-pound humans grow inside of him for nine months and then rip open his vagina. Zeke sat silently trying to forget the last thought he had.

After finishing their food, Gloria drove Zeke to the airport. As she pulled up to the curb, Zeke jumped out and waved. Before Gloria could depart, Zeke raised his hand for her to wait. He opened the door and moved over to her. He gave her a quick peck on the cheek and told her he loved her. Gloria smiled and began to think about Cirque du Soleil.

"Transcontinental flight 71 now boarding for Tony Bennett, I Left My Heart In San Francisco International Airport, the loud speaker blared in Zeke's ear as he walked through the sliding doors leading into the airport. He immediately ran to the end of the line for the security check. He pulled out his boarding pass he had printed from his computer and got out his driver's license as well. He stood behind an elderly couple that looked like they had just arrived from 1920's Russia. They spoke in a foreign tongue which was fine by Zeke. He didn't want to try and follow along with some troubled couple's travel woes – their indistinguishable idiom ensured he didn't have to know the details.

Zeke stared at the line in front of him for what seemed like fifteen minutes without movement. He could see up in the distance what appeared to be the same man constantly removing his shoes to be placed in a container for one of the metal detecting devices. The line slowly moved and he began to shake with anger as he knew it was the same man again taking his shoes off. He was some sort of business man wearing a weird tweed jacket that looked completely out of style. But it couldn't be the same man. As he continued to inch closer he could see a young couple being interrogated by one of the security guards.

"What in the world could they be talking to that couple about?" Zeke half yelled.

The Russo-Turkish couple in front of him turned around with irritated expressions on their faces.

"Can you believe those security people? They're obviously a young couple going on their honeymoon. What kind of trouble could they cause – this is ridiculous."

The elderly couple smiled like they were looking at a crazy man and turned around. Zeke kept staring at what he thought was the same man again taking his shoes off. It looked like the same weird tweed jacket, but he could see this man had on a beret or whatever you call those hats that the Scottish farmers wear all the time. Zeke stared at his watch – it had been twenty minutes and he had only moved twenty-six feet.

"Transcontinental Flight 81 now boarding for Paris, Jerry Lewis International Airport."

Zeke again peered at the man who was taking his shoes off. This definitely was a different man. He had a tweed jacket but this man had gray hair and spectacles, or did the other man have gray hair and spectacles too? This could not be the same guy, Zeke agonized. For another twenty minutes he waited in line. Good thing he gave himself an hour cushion.

When Zeke finally arrived at the metal detector, one of the security guards asked him for his driver's license and boarding pass. Zeke obligingly handed it to the perky twenty-year old.

"Ah, let's see here. Mr. Martin. Are how you, sir?"

"Just fine."

"Has your luggage been with you during the entire time you have been at the airport?"

"Yes."

"No one has asked you to carry anything with you or in your luggage?"

"No."

"Have you or anyone you know have been in contact with any terrorist organization over the past two years?"

Zeke was a little troubled by the question. "Ah, no."

"Are you carrying any weapons or anything that could be used as a weapon?"

"Well, I guess you're about to find out, right?"

"I don't think the metal detector is working very well

today." the security guard leaned over to Zeke and whispered.

"WHAT!!!" Zeke practically yelled.

The security guard tried to get Zeke to calm down.

"Just kidding, sir. I'm just trying something new so I can ascertain more information about certain individuals coming into the airport."

"I'm not following."

"You see, if I tell people that the security system is not working correctly I can ask them more detailed questions about their background, and really find the criminals!"

"Hmmm, are you sure that's legal?"

"Probably not, but I'm going to do it anyway."

"And I wanted to work for the government," Zeke said sarcastically to himself, as he slipped his shoes off for the metal detector.

"Northbest Airlines, now boarding all rows for flight 500 to Dallas J.R Ewing International Airport."

"Oh, that's my flight, I'd better get going!"

"Hold on, sonny!" a gray haired lady in security uniform shouted, standing watch over the monitor as Zeke's bag went through the conveyor belt.

"There's something in here I need to look at a little more closely. Mike, can you take this gentleman's bag and make a thorough search, please?" The gruff lady, looking like a guard from some high-security prison, motioned to "Mike" to search the bag.

Mike looked like he had been a pro wrestler at one time. His girth was enough to intimidate anyone. He took Zeke's bag with one hand like he was picking up a sandwich, a sub mind you. He threw the bag down, unzipped the top and began to pour through Zeke's personal items. Underwear, t-shirts and other garments were strewn on to the counter.

"Northbest flight 500 is now boarding for Dallas J.R Ewing International Airport."

Zeke began to sweat and shake. He couldn't miss his flight. Missing his flight would mean rebooking, and that could take forever.

"Ah, Mike, could you hurry it up a bit?" Zeke said politely.

"I'll take my sweet time, Mister."

"Yes, but, Mike, I need to get on that flight that they are making announcements for."

"Oh I see. You're in a hurry and you'd like me just to zip up the bag. Is that right?"

"Ah yes, Mike, that would be great."

"Yah, I bet you think that would be great because you are probably hiding this . . ."

Mike swiftly pulled out an object and nearly hit Zeke with it.

"So, Mr. Passenger, what were you planning on doing with this?"

"Well, it's a battery charger for my cell phone."

Mike began to examine the cord more closely. "I see here that it was made in Indonesia. Do you know where Indonesia is Mr . . . . ?"

"Martin, Zeke Martin. And yes, Indonesia is an archipelago in Southeast Asia."

"Yes, and do you know what comes from Indonesia?"

Zeke tried to stay cool and calm, wishing he had a large

mallet with which he could neutralize the tall guard. This had to be the worst case of government bureaucracy he had every seen. Zeke grumbled an answer back.

"Umm, rubber, coffee and quite few other natural resources."

"Yah, well have you heard of the natural resource called Muslim fundamentalism?"

"You've got to be kidding!" Zeke tried to stare down the inept officer but to no avail.

"So who is your cell phone provider?"

"It's Moronian."

"How much do you pay?"

"How much do I pay? I pay fifteen dollars a month for unlimited calls."

"Wow, that's a great deal."

"Yah, it's a government rate."

"You're in the government? Okay, you're free to go."

Zeke slapped himself in the face trying to believe what had just happened. He regained his senses after security had pretty well taken them away and began to run to the gate. Meanwhile, behind a ticket-counter podium, a darkened shadow, in the form of Jimmy Tinzdale, giggled as he watched the frantic Zeke Martin try and get through security.

"Northbest flight 500 to Dallas is now in the final boarding stages. Everyone with boarding passes should now be on board."

Zeke huffed and puffed his way down the terminal. He had been a football player in college but had since paid little attention to his shape. Perhaps that was the reason some of the luster had been lost in his relationship with Gloria. Maybe he was just as responsible for the routine and going through the motions as she was. He knew it was true and he vowed to change that, but intentions didn't always translate into action.

He rounded the corner to gate 15 and could quickly see they were about to close the door.

"Wait!!! Hold that door!!!" Zeke screamed, at the top of his lungs.

The gate agent turned to see Zeke jogging toward her.

"Sorry, sir, but the plane has already pulled away from the gate."

"You're going to have to call them and have them come back to the gate!"

"I'm sorry, sir, but it's too late."

"Yes, but I'm with the government!" Zeke tried to use the same line that had worked for him back in the security checkpoint.

"Oh I'm sorry; I didn't recognize you, President Bush!" The gate agent along with some of her cohorts began to laugh.

Zeke grimaced and began to yell. "You had better get that plane back here. I'm on important government business!"

"Sorry, sir, but we gave your seat to Secret Agent 007!"

"WHAT?!!!" Zeke again screamed. Soon he lost complete control of himself. He began to spin around like he was an Olympic discus thrower. He then threw his bag high up toward the ceiling where it caught a piece of metal attached to the ducting system, splitting it at the bottom. A woman sitting directly underneath the projectile received a shower of Zeke's clothes and hygiene products.

"Is this an airport or an insane asylum?" he cried.

As he began to pick up his belongings he was greeted by Mike and other airport security.

"What seems to be the problem here . . . oh, Mr. Martin it's you."

"What happened?"

"I missed the flight because of your security check!"

"Oh, I am sorry, but if you had shown your government ID earlier you could have gotten right through."

Zeke rolled his eyes and immediately handed his boarding pass to the gate agent so she could rebook him. Several beers and five hours later, Zeke boarded his flight to Dallas via Orlando.

"TransParagon flight 45 now boarding for Oralando Mickey Mouse Airport."

Zeke was beginning to feel anything related to the government was a Mickey Mouse operation.

The next day Zeke rose from his bed at 6:30 AM, shaved, showered and quickly headed down to the continental breakfast they were having in the front lobby of the Daze Inn. With a bagel and a cup of coffee in hand, he walked next door to the Dallas Convention Center where the conference was being held.

"Hey, Zeke, great to see you again man! How's it going?" yelled an excited Steve Dardwinkteek.

"Hey, pretty good, Steve. How have you been?"

Steve Dardwinkteek was Zeke's counterpart in Phoenix.

Like Zeke he was from the Deep South and the two had met at a similar conference five years earlier.

"Zeke, hey, I'll show you over to the check-in table where you can get your materials and ID badge."

"Great, Steve," Zeke said, with a moronic smile. He was truly glad to see one of his own kind. By own kind meaning anyone who wasn't Minnesotan. Minnesotans were beginning to wear a bit thin on him as of late and "Minnesota Nice" seemed to be turning into "Minnesota Ice," with the cool reception he was receiving for his investigation.

He and Steve caught up on what each other had been doing, and Zeke was happy to hear that Steve was quite content with his work in Phoenix. He didn't appear to have some of the same trials and tribulations that Zeke was having. The two sat together in the front row as the conference got underway.

"Good morning, everyone," said a rather dour looking man who wore thick glasses and was sporting a gray suit that looked like it had been saved in some warehouse since the 1950s. The speaker then began to bang into the microphone as he asked if the audience could hear him. With a large speaker behind him, feedback began to fill the auditorium, and as he continued to bang the vibration of sound caused many to cover their ears in pain. The speaker began to grimace and plug his ears with his fingers. He appeared to almost sway from the reverb that was causing the entire building to vibrate.

"My name is Seymour Sledge, and I am from the home office in Washington DC. Good morning to you and welcome to the fabulous city of Dallas."

Seymour, who appeared a little ill at ease and not quite comfortable with public speaking, coughed quietly into his hand and then took a sip of water from a nearby glass.

"Well, well, well, I think you will find we have a very exciting conference lined up for you over the next couple of days, with a couple of fabulous guest speakers," Seymour continued, in a monotone voice that sounded more robotic than human.

"Day one we will have various classes and workshops for you to attend. We will wrap up at about 5 PM, and reassemble here for dinner at 6 PM After a nice dinner of roast lamb, mashed potatoes, green peas with your choice of soft-drink or coffee, and dessert choices of apple pie or ice-cream . . . or both, he, he, he . . .

Seymour began to laugh incessantly, with everyone looking at each other trying to figure out the joke.

"Ah, yes, well, after dinner we will be entertained by the song stylings of Billy McGregor, the magic act of Shields and Sterns, and then our guest speaker . . . all the way from Washington of DC is our very own leader . . . John Llewellen."

With the rest of the audience, Zeke and Steve were nodding their heads in mutual approval.

"Tomorrow's agenda will be more of the same with classes and workshops throughout the day. We will conclude tomorrow's festivities with a dinner and entertainment with guest speaker Philip Bandersons from the Department of Forestry to tell us how we can better work together with his group."

Seymour next switched on a projector that beamed a PowerPoint slide onto a large screen for everyone to view. It was the schedule for the day's seminars.

"Alright, everyone, if you will turn your attention to the screen above, I will go over today's seminars. As per usual everyone is free to attend whichever seminar appeals to them. At 8 AM, we have the following . . . In the Cascade Room we have "Road Reclassification" with Jill Penningsburgh. In the Tropical Room we have "Gravel Repair" with Daven McCluster. In the Avalanche Room we have "Interstate Carriage Regulatory Updates" with John St. John. At 9 AM, in the Kona Room we have "Freeway Conversion" with Philip Wineriver . . ."

"Steve, let's head over to the Avalanche Room. I need to get some updates."

"You and me both."

The two smiled and nodded their heads in unison.

The two men hurriedly ran from the main meeting floor over to the Avalanche room.

John St. John was a very large man. Born in Jamaica he had nearly gone pro in cricket and soccer. The lure of the highway was more of an attraction to him, and the roads in Jamaica were the stuff legends were made of. He had once found a stranded Bob Marley on the road from Kingston to Montego Bay. St. John had been on a road inspection when he came upon the fatigued reggae star.

St. John gave him and his family a lift to the nearest gas station and was regaled with tales of the early days of the Wailers, "ganja" Haile Selassie and Ethiopia. Bob hoped to have a concert one day in Ethiopia, and invited St. John.

St. John himself had a cut a number of demos for his reggae band when he was only sixteen, but it was his encounter with Bob Marley six years later that convinced him of the importance of quality highways and quality related road services.

It was at a similar conference in Montego Bay seven years earlier that St. John had met Zeke. Zeke was from the south, but he was no hick. Zeke mentioned to St. John that he was a fan of the Wailers and Eric Clapton. Zeke was himself a humble bluesman, picking up his fender Stratocaster every once and a while to crank out some tasty licks. St. John was so impressed with Zeke's guitar work that he invited him to join him and his reggae/steel band for the gala at the conference closing evening. Zeke at that time had a habit of bringing his guitar with him on the road to keep him occupied. It was a night Zeke would never forget, and St. John made him an honorary Rastafarian.

"Brother Zeke!!!"

"John!!!"

The two men embraced much to the surprise of Steve Dardwinkteek.

"You two know each other?"

"Yah, we go back a ways Brother Zeke and I!" St. John bellowed in a deep and happy laugh. "This boy has the soul of a Rasta man! He be real heavy when 'e playin' that guitar."

Steve was a bit stunned to see his fellow southerner being grabbed by the huge man from Jamaica who could easily be confused with a defensive lineman from the Minnesota Norsemen.

"Hey, Zeke, let's get this seminar rollin' and we'll talk later."

"Sounds good, John . . . knock 'em dead."

With that St. John made his way to the front of the conference room where he immediately flicked on a switch to an overhead projector.

Zeke and Steve grabbed two vacant chairs at the back of the room and began to look through some manuals and other reading materials that had been laid out for attendees.

"Good morning, ladies and gentleman, welcome to Interstate Carriage Regulations Update. I'm John St. John and I'm with the Department of Highways Regulatory staff based in Washington DC."

St. John had come to the United States when he turned eighteen to attend the Baton Rough Institute of Road Sciences. Zeke and St. John didn't know it at the time, but it was St. John who kicked a winning 53 yard field goal in the last three seconds to give BRI a 23 to 20 victory over Zeke's Coastal Alabama team. St. John had majored in Highway regulations with a minor in music – he would have been in the pep band had it not been for his terrific kicking skills. Upon graduation from BRI, St. John went on to graduate school at Georgetown's famous Clifford Young School of Highway Analysis. His final thesis paper was on "Road Processes and Analysis from Ancient Rome to Modern Day Los Angeles."

With St. John's international experience in Jamaica, he was a shoe-in at the department in Washington upon graduation. He never looked back once hired by the government, quickly rising up the ranks within the department to where he finally became a field supervisor. His work took him everywhere in the world, and his name was respected within the world of highway and freeway management.

"Ladies and gentlemen, the area I want to focus on today during our short time together is the Hackins-McMurphy law of 1951. If you turn to page one in your manual you will see the entire law as it was written back in 1951. I've extracted several paragraphs that I'd like you to take a look at and see if it might be applicable to you in your home state."

St. John moved over to a nearby table, where he sat with one foot perched on top of a large box that looked like it had been used to carry the manuals.

"All right, and the first paragraph that I've extracted reads as follows: 'It is recognized that certain regulations pertaining to highway safety may be interpreted at a state level and may be instituted as that state sees fit. Along with this, states may also interpret certain driving techniques and training requirements at their own discretion. The U.S. Department of Highway safety understands that driving conditions and requirements in California may be different than those in Kentucky. It is with this knowledge that the Hackins-McMurphy Act acknowledges each state's own autonomy when it comes to highway safety."

St. John immediately popped up and switched off the overhead. He then began to pace back and forth slowly while repeating the regulation in a deep Jamaican accent. People began to imagine swaying palms on some isolated Jamaican beach with cries of "Hey, Mon" coming from the local merchants. A beautiful breeze, laden with coconut and lime, would swirl through their nostrils as they listened to Peter Tosh – it was intoxicating.

"All right, if everyone could put away their Caribbean fantasies for a moment, let's concentrate on what this regulation means for us all, shall we?"

Zeke was a step ahead of St. John. He knew immediately what this regulation meant for Minnesota. This had given the highway barons of the 1950s the opportunity to create their own infrastructure and rules for the road. It was no wonder that Minnesotans had a style of driving that was different from anywhere in the world that Zeke had been to. St. John continued.

"Because of this statute, ladies and gentlemen, it is incumbent upon you to review the addendums that local authorities in your state may or may not have added to various traffic laws. If you take anything away from this seminar, it is to remember that laws that you think are commonsense and well known throughout the U.S. may in fact be little known to the driving population you oversee."

Zeke nodded his head in amazement. It was true, and he couldn't wait to hop back on that plane to Minneapolis (and St. Paul), to reread the traffic laws of Minnesota.

After a momentous couple of days at the seminar, Zeke was feeling a renewed belief that he could right the wrongs of the past and bring a new order to Minnesota driving. At the closing ceremony for the conference he was invited to play "Curly" in the Department of Highways rendition of "Oklahoma." It was a riot, as a local Dallas orchestra was brought in to back the players. Zeke was happy that female lead was played by Phyllis Blackwell, a very attractive highway detective from the Baltimore branch. She had dark sultry hair and a figure to tell the day by. The annual conference always ended with a musical production. The previous year had been Grease and the year before that it was Hair without the nudity.

The idea of a closing musical was the brainchild of Seattle Director Bill Collingshead who thought it would be a great way of doing team-building amongst the branches. On the first day of the conference everyone would get their notebook, along with the script for the final night's production.

This year's production went off without a hitch, with Zeke stealing the show as always.

"Zeke, you should have been in show biz!" blustered Amanda Sizewater, director from the western region in LA.

"No, no . . . gravel and cement oozes through my veins, I'm afraid."

Amanda starred at the ceiling unsure of what to say.

"Anyway, I think I'll go over and grab some prime rib before its all gone."

Again Amanda was staring off into space.

It had been a good night and a good conference, but Zeke knew his work was just beginning. Trying to slog his way through the bureaucratic jungle of St. Paul was going to be difficult, if not impossible. It would take cunning, skill and perhaps even walking the edge between what was considered legal and illegal.

CHAPTER 4

After Zeke got into the Minneapolis and St. Paul airport, he immediately hailed a cab to go to the capital. He needed to go to the main office and try and access the original manual for all of the state traffic laws. It was a large book and only portions of it were printed online for people to browse on the Internet.

As he raced through the rotunda of the capital building, he almost took a spill as he reached for the door to the Department of Transportation. He tried to gather himself as he was huffing and puffing his way over to the receptionist.

"Hi, Gladys!" he said, on the verge of a coronary.

"Oh hi, Zeke! What can I do you for?" the kindly spectacled admin asked.

"I need the 'State Manual for Traffic Laws and Addendums' please, Gladys."

Gladys did a spit take as she drew a sip of her piping hot coffee. Zeke tried to help her mop up the papers on her desk but she slapped his hand out of the way.

"No, no, that's not necessary, Zeke," Gladys said

frantically, as if to apologize for her own clumsiness.

"Gladys, what's the matter? You're shaking . . . are you okay?"

"Yes, yes, fine. It's just that I've never had such a request before."

"You haven't . . . why?"

"I don't know. I suppose it's just that everyone uses the field manual."

"Yes, but the field manual doesn't contain all of the laws as well as the addendums."

Gladys nodded silently as she finished mopping up her coffee. She finally regained her composure and sat down. "I'm going to need to make a quick call to the director. I know the manual is kept under lock and key somewhere."

Zeke was puzzled. Why all the fuss just to take a look at the 'State Manual for Traffic Laws and Addendums'? Something wasn't right.

"Um, Director Waxhead? Yes, it's Gladys in reception. Yes, sir, I know it's your lunch break, but . . . you're what? You're having a soufflé. Yes, sir, I'm sorry to . . . what? You also are having shrimp scampi with Cream of Broccoli soup. Hmm, uh ah, yes I see, and you're having Boston Cream Pie for dessert. Yes, yes, sir, I see that it is interrupting your gourmet meal but I have one of your field investigators here, Zeke Martin. Yes, sir, I'll tell him that. I'll tell him that he's a hick from the sticks." She turned to him. "He's just joking, Zeke." Then she returned to her call. "Anyway, yes, Zeke needs to take a look at the 'State Manual for Traffic Laws and Addendums.'"

With that, Gladys immediately pulled the phone away

from her head as the director began to scream. She slowly tried to put the phone back near her ear but again the screaming came pouring out of the phone for all in the office to hear.

"Ah, yes, sir, I know. Um, yes, okay, I see. Yes I see, I will let him know." The stunned receptionist placed the phone down and shook her head like she was trying to get water out of her ears.

"I'm sorry, Zeke, but you need to provide a written request as to why you would like to review the manual. The director said there is a three week minimum turn around before they will respond to your request."

Zeke was dumfounded. "Written request . . . three week turn-around? This is ludicrous!"

"I know, but that is what the director said."

Zeke turned around is stunned silence, his mouth agape. Of all the bureaucratic messes he had to be apart of, this was by far the worst he had ever seen. He could not imagine how anything could get done in the capital with all of the bureaucratic red tape one has to follow.

Zeke shook his head, quickly turned around back to the receptionist and grabbed the 180F–12 written request form which Gladys held out in anticipation that he would reconsider and need.

Zeke immediately hailed a cab and sat silently in disbelief all the way home. The cabbie played Somali jazz in the cab, but it wasn't enough to cheer him up.

When he arrived home, Gloria had his plate of hot Hamburger Helper waiting for him. As he gave her an unconsciousness peck on the cheek, he dropped his briefcase and jacket on the floor by the entryway and immediately plopped himself down for his dinner. Silently he moved over to the frig to grab himself a Lennie. He didn't normally drink a lot of beer, but tonight he felt like he would have a couple. The stress of the case and the apparent scandal along with it was starting to wear on him.

As he began to devour his Hamburger Helper he noticed Gloria looking out the kitchen window at the setting sun. The golden light on her face seemed to capture the silky skin that seemed to escape her the past few years. Her pensive brow reminded him of the young, enthusiastic student she was at Alabama Coastal.

He knew why he loved Gloria – she was kind and loving, and deep down had a spirituality that attracted him. The years were starting to show, but he knew that life was more than physical beauty; it was about friendship and having a soul-mate. Gloria was that soul-mate. She didn't have the physical beauty of Malaysia, but she had an inner beauty that was difficult to find.

"How was your day?" Zeke asked, not really caring what the answer would be, but wanting to know what was on her mind that would put her in such deep thought.

"Oh, uh, pretty good. I did a little Christmas shopping for the kids, and met Betty for lunch."

"Sounds busy. Anything in particular you're thinking about?"

"Thinking about?"

"Yah, you look a little deep in thought."

Gloria was a little surprised. As far as she knew it was a look that she was often wearing. Although a housewife,

Gloria prided herself on her intellect. She had minored in philosophy at Alabama Coastal and was an avid reader. With Zeke busy with his work so often, Socrates and Descartes were her best friends, save Betty of course. But Betty could not stand up to Aristotle or Kafka or Kierkegaard. Betty was a nice tennis buddy and bridge partner, but neither she nor Zeke could fill the intellectual void she was sometimes desperate to fill.

"That's funny," she said.

"What?"

"I never thought you noticed when I'm deep in thought."

"Why do you say that?"

"Well, because this is the first time in years that you've asked me what I'm thinking about."

Zeke was silent. It was true. As relationships go, theirs was similar to every other one in the world. As years go on, each partner becomes less curious and begins to take the other for granted.

"Um, I guess your right. I guess I've been a bit busy and my mind gets a little preoccupied."

"Do you ever think I get busy and 'a little preoccupied'?"

Zeke was again silent. It was difficult to admit when you were not picking up your end of the relationship. It was easy to make work an excuse not to engage your partner in communicating, and he knew he was as guilty as the next guy.

"Yes, I guess you do get busy. Look, I know I get a little preoccupied with my job but I feel like sometimes I can really make a difference."

"Really, how?"

Zeke had to think what he meant by his comment. It was easy to say but not easy to convey the reality of his job. He would tell Gloria about all of his problems when they were newlyweds, but over the years it became more and more difficult to explain the complexities of road management, but he guessed he was guilty of not making the effort.

"Well, sometimes the rules and the regulations that are made to ensure safety are . . . are . . ."

"Yes?"

Zeke was deep in thought. He was seeing Gloria for the first time in years. She was not only internally beautiful but physically beautiful as well. She wasn't Malaysia St. Croix but she was his wife, his soul-mate and, even better, his best friend.

"Do you remember the Florida R&E (Road Engineering) game back in '81?"

Gloria broke her gaze at the sunset and sat down at the kitchen table. "Yah."

"Remember how Florida R&E was up 23 to 17 with 45 seconds to go?"

"Yah."

"Remember how we tried to throw against their defense on the first three downs, and they seemed invincible?"

"Of course. Don't forget I was the lead cheerleader. Remember the cool cheer I came up with? 'Socrates is great! Aristophanes is cool! Florida R&E is being taken to school!!!'"

"Ah yah, I do, that was a good one. Anyway, I thought we were going to lose for sure. I had lost my confidence and it was 4th down and 50 yards to go for a touchdown. I remember I looked over at you as you were twirling around like some sort of wayward juggernaut. You had that bright, confident smile that said, 'I believe in you, Zeke.' Well, that was all I needed. I called for the flea-flicker play where I immediately threw it to Harry Shackleton who then immediately threw it back to me. It didn't fool R&E too much, but it gave them enough hesitation that I was able to hurl it sixty yards in the air to Roy Muggins in the corner of the end zone for the victory. Remember how the whole crowd went wild, and I was raised on the shoulders of the players? Remember the after-game party?"

Zeke smiled as he could see the whole thing played out again in his mind's eye. He felt that Gloria was being transported back to.

"And your point is?" she asked.

"Ah . . . I can't remember."

As Zeke grinned broadly over his past glories, the phone began to ring, snapping him back to the present.

"Ah, yes. Just a moment please." Gloria walked the portable phone over to Zeke.

"Martin!" Zeke yelled into the phone, upset that someone had interrupted his journey back into memory lane.

"Mr. Martin. My name is . . . uh, let's just say I am someone with some information you might be interested in."

"I'm listening."

"Well, it's a little sensitive. I'd like to meet you somewhere in private. How 'bout you meet me at the parking lot behind the Bull's-eye store at the Southdale shopping mall in thirty minutes?"

"What's this all about?"

"It's very important I meet you. It's about the Shakopee case you are investigating. That's all I can say."

The phone went dead. Zeke began to scratch his head. The voice sounded familiar but who could it be? Was this some sort of a set-up? Did someone have it in for him? Would they possibly try and harm him? Nothing was a certainty these days. It could be some weirdo trying to rob him, or do some other kind of harm to him. But he did reference the Shakopee case, and he needed every bit of information he could dig up.

With one last gulp of Hamburger Helper and a quick peck on Gloria's cheek, he was out the door and back into his faithful pick-up, soon squealing down the deserted streets of Burnsville. Several deer on a secluded hill stood and watched.

If there was one thing that Zeke detested it was shopping – even being near a shopping mall made him nervous. Shopping malls were like large endless mazes that most self-respecting men could be trapped in for hours with no hope of finding an exit. This at times even proved to be another thorn in Gloria's side, as she loved to shop. Gloria was an intellectual, but she still loved the thirteen-hour sales at Lacy's. She might enjoy a good Voltaire novel or play, but Versace was also on her mind, and it was all she could do to drag Zeke out every once and a while to take a look at the latest fashions which he could care less about.

As Zeke pulled into the parking lot behind Bull's Eye's, he noticed there were very few cars around – it must be closing time for most of the stores. As he drove around he could see a man standing by his car in the rear of the lot. He was wearing a trench coat and smoking a cigarette. Zeke cruised by slowly and nodded to the man who returned his gesture with a tap on the brim of his hat. He wore an old-fashioned derby which was completely out of style. By the man's appearance however, he was probably in his seventies and had owned the hat since the 1950s.

Zeke parked and slowly walked up to the man. He walked cautiously looking around to see if anyone else were around. "I'm Zeke Martin. Are you the man who wanted to see me?"

The man peered at Zeke with a hardened glare that resembled that of a paroled convict. He threw away the cigarette and nodded his head to Zeke. "Yah, I'm the m . . . argh..ah%^*#@ . . ."

The man began to choke and then started to cough. It was an incessant hacker's cough – a smoker's cough that was bordering on emphysema.

"Hey, are you okay?" Zeke began to pat the man on the back hoping that such a procedure would relieve the man of his ailment.

"Sorry about that. Gotta give those things up, hey?"

"Ah, that might be wise. And so why did you call me out here?"

The man looked slowly to the left and then to the right. He then looked behind him and then up toward the sky. "Can't be too sure who might be listening to us, you know."

"You said you had some information about the Shakopee case – what is it?"

"Yah, I've got some information – information that most people would probably pay for."

The man began to look off into the distance like he was expecting some sort of gratuity before he would divulge. Zeke caught his drift, but as a rule didn't carry too much cash with him. He slowly slipped his hand into his pocket and pulled out what appeared to be money and placed it into the man's hand. The man took a quick peak.

"A dollar? You're giving me a lousy dollar and some lint?"

"It's all I got. Well, I'm mean. I've got some loose change here and some gum. Oh wait! Here's a five."

The man rolled his eyes toward the sky and began to shake his head. "It's a good thing I've have concern for my fellow man."

"Well I'm sorry. They just don't pay government employees like they used to."

"Don't I know it. In fact that's why I'm here. I used to work in the Department of Transportation. I used to do your job years ago."

Zeke looked the man up and down, trying to determine if it were true what he was saying. He could always spot a Highway Inspector from miles away. There is something in their blood, something different that drove an inspector. It was easy to say you were in the Highways Division as an inspector, but to really mean it you had to know your stuff. Zeke began to walk around the "inspector," inspecting him for inspector-type qualities.

"I see. Let me ask you a question then. What year was the first Roman road built in England?"

The man was silent but gave Zeke a confident look. He nodded at Zeke as if to accept the challenge he was throwing down. "The first Roman road in England was built in 43 AD."

Zeke walked around the "inspector" like they were doing a slow dance, not letting him know whether his answer was right or wrong, his face holding a cold stare.

"What year was the first freeway built in Los Angeles?"

The "inspector" smiled.

"Nineteen forty-nine. C'mon, got anything harder than that?"

Zeke quickly shot back, "Name the building material used to create the overpass on Interstate 35, 35.6 miles north of Des Moines Iowa?"

The "inspector" smiled again. This time he really had to think, and began to circle around Zeke like he had done previously. "It was a synthetic bond of limestone, gravel and chemcrete."

Zeke nodded his head in agreement. "You do know your stuff. I think I can trust you. Let me know what you got."

The man began to shed some light on the 169 and 494 interchange in Eden Prairie. This bottleneck had been responsible for multiple accidents, and there were no plans to change it. His buddy, Simon Callahan, was in charge of the layout in that part of the city, and would be pushing for funding to remove traffic lights at either end of 169 as it passed over 494, to allow for better flow of traffic.

Back in 1978, Simon did not show up for work one day. The "inspector" became suspicious and asked Waxhead what had happened to Callahan. Waxhead created some story that Callahan had been reassigned to the federal office in Guam. When he had tried to contact Callahan in Guam there was no listing for him there. He had tried to contact his family but they had been "relocated." It was all very suspicious to the "inspector."

The next day while patrolling the interchange, the "inspector" driving down from St. Louis Park in the north down to Eden Prairie, spotted a crew installing a sign near the interchange. The sign read "Plan on Heavy Congestion." This was a puzzle. Why would they "plan" on having congestion, and not just remove the traffic lights? He later recalled a conversation he overheard in the capital building between Waxhead and Harry Steel of ABC towing. Waxhead was laughing and said in reference to the 169/494 interchange, "We've got us a real money-maker there."

Zeke was horrified when he heard this. How could this be? How could government officials have created such a system of corruption? He walked over to a bush and threw up. The "Inspector" walked over and patted him on the back.

"I can't believe it!" Zeke cried, as he wiped some vomit from his chin. "How could someone take something so sacred as our highways and roads, our right to good transportation, and just throw it away like that for money?"

"I don't know, Zeke. Men, sometimes good men, can be corrupted quickly when it comes to a good payday. Anyway, I'm missing The Price Is Right. I'll see you later."

Zeke watched as the "Inspector" quickly sped away in his car, leaving him alone in the empty parking lot. Zeke was still in shock. He began to shake his head, starting to believe that this was the raving of an old, bitter highway inspector who was just trying to gain some glory in his retirement.

There was no way these allegations could be true. But Zeke aimed to find out.

CHAPTER 5

The next day a dejected Zeke flung his brief case onto his desk and walked over to a nearby table to pour himself a cup of coffee.

"Something the matter, Zeke?" Malaysia wondered aloud.

Zeke took a sip of coffee then wiped an ounce of coffee grounds from his chin. He hated the way Malaysia made coffee, but he wasn't about to tell her.

"Oh, it's this whole Shakopee case. I feel like the state is really impeding my investigation."

"Why do you say that?"

"Well, for example, last night I go to pick up the 'State Manual for Traffic Laws and Addendums,' and old man Waxhead won't let me see it. He said I have to fill a written permission form and that it will take a minimum of three weeks before I can see it."

Malaysia looked pensive. She took a sip of coffee and quickly dabbed a napkin on her chin to remove the stray coffee grounds. She sat back and then authoritatively removed her glasses. The whole process began to arouse Zeke. When she removed her glasses her beautiful blue-green eyes somehow seemed even more beautiful. Perhaps the glasses she wore diminished the brilliance of her eyes? Something seemed different, but either way, glasses or no glasses, he could stare at Malaysia for hours.

"Zeke, you know that any government is a bureaucratic mess. Look who I worked for – NASA! I had to get written permission just to get a cup of coffee. You can't let government processes slow you down. That is what has made this country great . . . those who didn't let the government or certain laws keep them from doing great things. Look at J. Edgar Hoover. Do you think he followed the law all the time? How d'yah think he got all that dirt on JFK and all his mistresses? And how about Richard Nixon? Do you think the President of the United States would let a little thing like burglary prevent him from breaking into the Democratic headquarters at Watergate?"

Both were silent as they thought through the last statement.

"The point is, Zeke, people have lost their lives, and we need to do something about it. There also might be corruption involved here, and we need to find out."

"What are you proposing?"

"I think we need to go down there tonight and break into the capital and take that manual."

Zeke was dumfounded that Malaysia could even think of such a thing. But there was more to Malaysia then met the eye. She had done a lot during her tenure at NASA, and it was clear she had a worldliness about her. She spoke four languages and had done a lot of diplomatic work for NASA in Spain, Greece, Russia and the Channel Islands. Maybe she was the right person to consult on this. She knew the inner workings of government which Zeke had tried to avoid like the plague. Maybe she was the person who knew just what to do.

"Are you sure, Malaysia, that's the right thing to do?"

"I'm positive. I know men like Waxhead. They are here to ride on the taxpayers' dollars. They serve no useful purpose to society other than to drain its resources. I would go as far to say that he is on the take. There is probably some business that needs his support, and they've paid him off."

It all seemed too much to believe, but Zeke trusted Malaysia. She had seen a lot during her career, and that was probably why she had been demoted on a number of occasions. She wasn't the type to just let things ride – she would speak up and make herself be heard.

"Well, okay. How 'bout I pick you up at your place at midnight? I'll bring some equipment . . . I think I know how to get at that manual."

"Great. I'll be waiting with bells on."

No sooner had Zeke and Malaysia confirmed their plans, when Jimmy Tinzdale walked into the office. He grunted to Zeke and Malaysia after each had greeted him with a happy salutation. Jimmy walked over to his desk and started to ruffle through a myriad of papers that had piled up.

"You two look like the cats that caught the canaries."

"You mean the cat that caught the canary?"

"No I mean the *cats* that caught the *canaries!*" Jimmy snapped back at Malaysia. "I can tell you never went to school. It would be plural if I am referring to more than one of you. Correct?" Jimmy said, puffing out his chest.

Malaysia shrugged her shoulders and pretended to do some work. It had been adversarial as of late between Jimmy and the other members of the office. It was clear Jimmy Tinzdale was the eyes and ears of Waxhead, which was a rather unpleasant image to conjure up, but it was important not to let him in on too much of the branch business. Jimmy's tone became friendlier as he began to fish around for information.

"So what are you two up to today?" he queried both Zeke and Malaysia.

"Oh nothing," Zeke said, as he also pretended to do paperwork.

"Well, I'm going at to that new action film tonight starring Red Rockhead – 'The Gladiator and the Ninja'. Anyone want to come along? Malaysia?" Jimmy asked, with a broad grin that gave him the appearance of the Cheshire Cat.

She smiled coyly at Zeke. "Sorry, I've got a date tonight."

Zeke looked up at Malaysia with a blank stare, relieved that her back was turned to Jimmy.

Jimmy again applied his moronic grin. "Date, huh? Who with, may I inquire?"

"No you may not. But I can tell you one thing, it will be a lot more stimulating than going to see the 'The Gladiator and the Ninja'!" She giggled to herself as she said the title.

"Oh I see, it's probably a little too intellectual for you?"

Both Zeke and Malaysia burst into laughter, quite aware of the intellectual prowess, or lack thereof in the film.

"Are you kidding? The film is either for ten-year-old boys or someone with mental disabilities!"

"Oh, how so, Ms. Einstein?"

"Well first off, Ninjas did not exist in the first century . . ."

"Could have. You don't know that for sure."

"Ninjas were a group of warriors that were created in nineteenth century Japan. But aside from that, the plot is moronic."

"I find the plot very inspiring."

"What? It's about a Ninja and a geisha girl who gets shipwrecked in first century Rome – Rome, remember is landlocked. Anyway, the girl is kidnapped by Alexander the Great, who by the way is Greek and lived over three hundred years earlier! The plot continues with a Roman Gladiator, selected by Caesar Giovanni, to aid the Ninja in finding the girl. The girl is rescued in Spartucul, wherever and whatever that is, where she becomes the queen of the recently arrived Mongol horde!"

"Yah, isn't that great?!!!"

"Yah, if you like completely unrealistic, horribly made movies."

"You're just jealous because you don't know anything about history."

Zeke began to laugh uncontrollably at Jimmy's comments. "Look, Jimmy, the film was made by a glue-sniffing Dutchman who dropped out of primary school and has no clue about history."

"Yah, but it's still good."

Jimmy thought for a minute as he eyed Zeke and

Malaysia up and down. He stood up and walked between their two desks.

"Hmmm, I wonder if that date Malaysia is talking about is with you, Zeke?"

"Are you crazy?" Malaysia blurted out.

"Geez, don't get so defensive, Malaysia. I mean after all, you two sure spend a lot of time together."

"Jimmy, why don't you go have lunch with your uncle Harry or something – something a lot more productive than this."

"Oh, I'm doing something productive all right. I'm keeping my eye on you two and this office. I can tell when someone is trying to upset the fruit-cart. When someone is maybe unhappy with their job? Maybe they want some action so they try and create an issue? Know what I mean, Zeke?"

"Applecart."

"Applecart?"

"You said fruit-cart, when it's actually applecart."

Jimmy Tinzdale stood up and walked back toward his desk. Clearly he wasn't going to intimidate Zeke or Malaysia, but as he said, he was going to keep his eyes on things around the office.

At precisely Midnight, Zeke met Malaysia at her town-home in Eden Prairie. She wore a tight fitting black sweater with what appeared to be matching black tights and boots – probably not the most stealthy when it came to spy-wear. It looked like she had done this before. Zeke was a little embarrassed, as he was wearing a plaid shirt and jeans with brown work boots. Malaysia looked around and then motioned for Zeke to come through the front entrance.

"Wow, great place you have here, Malaysia. Did you decorate this yourself?"

"I did have a little help from my mom. She's the artistic one in our family."

"Oh really? Was she a professional?"

"Yes, she studied under Picasso."

"Really? Pablo Picasso?"

"No, Billy Picasso."

Zeke did a double take but took Malaysia's word for it. The town-home had the look and feel that Zeke imagined it would have. It was a tropical Asian feel with a lot of floral arrangements, including small palm trees intermingled with furniture made of wicker and teak.

"Can I offer you a drink?"

"Ah, I don't think that would be wise right now. I better have my wits about me."

"Even a teensy little drink to build your courage?"

"Ah, maybe you're right. Maybe a quick shot of something to settle my nerves."

Malaysia walked over to the kitchen where she had a tray laid out with a bottle and a couple of shot glasses.

"This is a liqueur from Thailand that I think you'll love. It has a sweet and woody bite to it."

Zeke nodded his head in agreement, wondering what he was getting himself into. Malaysia poured him a half a shot glass and he immediately downed it in one gulp.

"Geez, big boy, you're supposed to sip it."

Zeke licked his lips and offered his glass to be filled

again. It was a very tasty liqueur and he could not quite remember if he had ever tasted anything like it. It was like some sort of cross between molasses, butter and sugar cane, yet with a bitter woody flavor like Malaysia had explained.

"You better go easy on this stuff."

Malaysia took her shot while she poured more for Zeke. He immediately took another swig and soon found himself hallucinating that he was on some Tahitian beach and Malaysia was wearing a bikini.

"Wow, this is powerful stuff. Is it legal?"

"Are you kidding? It's made on the streets of Bangkok!"

"Oh," Zeke said numbly, as he began to stagger around the room. "We better get going, Malaysia," he said, trying to feel around for his lips.

"I'm right behind you," said an equally incoherent Malaysia.

After driving in circles in the Townhouse parking lot for twenty-five minutes, Malaysia finally convinced Zeke that she should get her sister to drive them.

Malaysia's sister Bermuda, named after the island where she was conceived on her parents' second anniversary holiday, lived in the town-home next to Malaysia.

"Wow, Malaysia, I didn't know you had a sister."

"Oh yah, I actually have two brothers as well. Zaire and Trenton."

"Boy, your parents have been all over the world."

While driving over to St. Paul, Malaysia pulled out a can.

"What's that?" Zeke queried.

"It's shoe polish. We're going to need to put this on our faces. Don't want to be recognized. Right?"

Zeke agreed, and began to smear the black shoe polish over his face.

After Bermuda dropped them both off on the capital steps in plain view of everyone around, she headed off into the dark St. Paul streets, planning to return in an hour.

Zeke and Malaysia immediately ran around the back and found the cellar access to the building. Zeke held his ID badge to the scanner near the entrance, and the door immediately clicked open. They walked down a brightly lit hallway and then took an elevator up to the reception floor. Zeke again used his ID to enter the reception area. Now would be the hard part – the hallway to the records room was adorned with several surveillance cameras.

Avoiding the hallway with the surveillance cameras, they went over to the men's bathroom. Once inside the bathroom, they knew what to do. Malaysia clumsily climbed onto Zeke's shoulders. Zeke, still intoxicated with the Thai liqueur, did his best to keep her on his shoulders. Malaysia produced a screwdriver and quickly removed the air vent cover to the ceiling.

Zeke's head began to pound as he staggered under the weight of Malaysia. He prided himself on being an ex-collegiate quarterback and did his best to go to the gym at least twice a week to keep himself fit. With Malaysia now working in the office, there was a subconscious need to try and go at least three times a week.

As Malaysia released the vent cover, he gave out a loud shriek as the grating on the cover banged off his chin and onto his foot. Luckily his face was numb, but just the sight of the cover hitting him was enough to make him cry out.

Malaysia, oblivious to the pain she had subjected him to, immediately grabbed onto the edges of the hole where the cover once was, and pulled herself up into the ductwork. Zeke threw a plastic bag up to her and she began to shimmy down the series of vents that led to the rotunda area.

Once there, she started to unscrew the bolts that held the vent cover at the end of the duct tunnel and removed it. She then removed a paint spray gun and began to spray over the surveillance cameras.

A nearby guard was sitting in front of a row of surveillance monitors. Each monitor displayed streams of black paint jetting out from the vent that Malaysia had positioned herself in. Each jet of black paint hit its intended target, and soon each monitor went black. It was pointless, however, as the guard was sound asleep.

Her work completed, Malaysia scurried back the way she had come and lowered herself down the hole into the men's bathroom. A rather eager Zeke was waiting for her as she began her descent. As Malaysia lowered herself down, she slipped slightly and began to fall – luckily Zeke was there to catch her. As he embraced her, a little more tightly than he had wanted to, he began to look into her eyes. Malaysia seemed to return his gaze and began to smile. Even with black shoe polished smeared over face, Malaysia looked beautiful. His heart began to pound and he felt light-headed, but he couldn't tell if it was the Thai liqueur or Malaysia – or maybe both.

"Ah . . . everything go okay up there?" Zeke managed to get out.

"Yah . . . Yah, everything went, ah, fine." Malaysia felt

Zeke's grasp and wasn't necessarily in a hurry for him to let go.

"Ah, well, I guess we better get over to the records room."

"That might be a good idea."

Slowly Zeke released his grasp of Malaysia, and he could feel his chest pounding to the point that he thought Malaysia could see it. He could feel his face was warm and probably bright red, but Malaysia wasn't letting on.

The two peered out of the door of the men's bathroom, looking around for any security. Then they slowly moved down the hallway hoping that Malaysia's spray paint would hold in place. As they made their way through the rotunda, they listened carefully for anyone who might be around. It was eerily silent and it seemed too good to be true that they had not encountered anyone yet.

As they crept through the large wooden door to the records room, they were immediately greeted by a tall steel door. Zeke had never been to the records room before, but knew there were several doors beyond the front door. He raised his hand to a scanner that detected his palm print and opened the large steel door. The next door was a large wooden one, like the one in front, and this time Zeke only needed his ID badge. That door too flung open and they walked into a darkened room that was not large but very tall. In each wall was shelving that housed what appeared to be millions of books. How would they ever find the manual they needed?

Luckily, there were ladders to reach the shelves. But these were not ordinary ladders, they were electric ladders.

There was one ladder for each wall. Each ladder had a stand that would go up the ladder with the press of a button. On the stand was a little control panel with a lever that allowed you to move the ladder to the left and to the right, as well as move up and down the ladder itself.

"Whoever created these things was a genius!" Zeke exclaimed.

Malaysia nodded, also impressed with the technology employed by the state. "Yah, this will help us quicken the process."

Taking separate walls, they each began to enjoy the quick ride up and down the ladders. Pretty soon they were both giggling from the effects of the Thai liqueur and the sensations of moving up and down the walls like they were test pilots. After an hour of swooshing up and down the electric ladders, Zeke and Malaysia found an area near the top of one of the walls that seemed to be getting them closer to their objective. Zeke could see that the area they had finally reached seemed to have manuals on regulations and other state laws.

"I think we're almost there!" he shouted.

Malaysia was in hot pursuit. The great thing about the ladders was that they could move from one wall to the other, on circular tracks. If you ran into one of the other ladders, you could simply push that one along as you moved yours.

"Great work, Zeke. Say, I hope you're not afraid of heights?" Malaysia shouted back up.

Zeke turned around and could see that he was several stories up, and perhaps near a hundred feet above the floor. He wasn't exactly afraid of heights, but the combination of operating machinery and the Thai liqueur made him a little unsure of himself.

"Wow, I didn't realize how high we were."

As he kept manipulating the ladder higher and higher, and toward the left-hand side of the wall, he finally came upon the manual he had been seeking.

"I found it!!!"

Just then the door to the records room burst open and the once-sleeping guard came charging in.

"Hey, you two, what are you doing here?"

Zeke almost dropped the manual. Malaysia nudged him and pointed to a vent at the top of the records room. They immediately accelerated their ladders up toward the vent.

"Hey, come back here!!!" the guard screamed, as he ran over to one of the other ladders. He jumped onto one of the stands and slammed the lever into high gear sending him on a high speed chase. The guard was obviously experienced at using the ladders as he seemed to be able to get more speed out of it than Zeke or Malaysia could.

"Malaysia, grab that manual on Minnesota Fishing and Hunting Regulations, I've got an idea."

It was all Malaysia could do to grab the huge manual. Zeke could see she was struggling with the monster book and immediately lowered himself down to where she was. With one mighty hand he grabbed it from her and motioned for her to follow him. They both accelerated to the very top of the records room where Zeke pushed the vent cover through. They both climbed through the hole and hoped they had enough time to escape.

As Zeke looked back through the hole, he could see the

guard in hot pursuit. It was a difficult angle but Zeke had been in many football games at Coastal Alabama that required him to throw passes at odd angles. As the guard accelerated toward the ceiling, Zeke took aim with the fishing and hunting manual at the control panel on the guard's ladder. With one quick flick of the wrist the manual went hurtling down toward the guard. It struck the lever perfectly, causing the ladder to stop instantly, sending the guard into the air.

As the guard came back down, the collar of his uniform caught onto the lever and locked into the "left" steering position. The guard who was helpless to do anything, was stuck on the ladder as it began to make laps around the room.

It wasn't until the next morning when there was a shift change that the hapless and dazed guard would be discovered still making laps around the room. There would have to be an inquiry into why two unidentified people had broken into the library for the Minnesota Fishing and Hunting Regulations, but at least the guards were pleased to know that the theft had been unsuccessful.

Everything went to plan the rest of the evening. Bermuda met them exactly an hour later and they were back in Shakopee by 1:30 AM. As Zeke walked Malaysia back to her door he began to feel the cold night air beginning to wake him out of his Thai liqueur haze.

"Well, that was an exciting evening to say the least."

"Do you always show a girl such a good time, Mr. Martin?" Malaysia said coyly.

"Uh . . ." Zeke became quiet, unsure what to say. "Yah,

stick around me young lady, and things will really start to get exciting."

He wanted to kick himself for saying that, but it slipped out. Malaysia nodded her head with a big grin and gave him a wink.

"Thanks, Zeke. I'll see you bright and early on Monday morning."

"Ah, yah, Malaysia. Sounds good. Good night."

Why was God doing this to him? Zeke muttered to himself as he got into his car. Of all the offices in the world, Malaysia St. Croix had to work in his.

CHAPTER 6

Zeke spent the rest of the weekend going over the manual, and seeing what he could find on merging laws in Minnesota. He grabbed a cup of hot coffee that his wife had habitually prepared for him every day. For some reason the coffee tasted especially good, almost restaurant quality. He always wondered how restaurants could prepare coffee so well. It was like restaurants, and only restaurants, had secret access to some incredibly rich coffee that was illegally smuggled in from Colombia – and stored only at restaurants, any restaurant. He wanted that Colombian contact – he was a coffee fanatic. Coffee though was not the only thing keeping him up at nights.

As he pored over the manual he finally came to what he thought he was looking for: section 1033, for regulation P177-38. The title was a little ominous. "Merging and Related Deletions." The section read as follows:

"Pursuit to Federal regulation Z-278-34B, the state of Minnesota hereby shall now and forthwith refrain from detailing and explaining to the general driving public on how and when to 'merge.' The definition of 'merge' shall mean to drive at a speed that allows you to change from one lane into another lane while not interfering with the other cars in the same lane that the driver is entering. Further definition of 'merge' is that the speed of the driver shall allow for him or her to enter the desired lane without causing the car behind them to slow, and shall not impact any cars in front of them. The driver should allow for one car length per each 10 miles an hour he or she is driving. For example, if the driver is at a speed of 50 miles an hour, upon entering the new lane there should be at least five car lengths between them and the car in back of them and the car in front of them.

"Pursuant to Federal regulation Z-278-34B, the state of Minnesota is no longer liable for any accidents caused by motorists when an accident occurs because of any merging. The state of Minnesota is no longer required to provide testing and information on merging."

"Those bastards!" Zeke screamed.

Gloria came running into the kitchen wondering what could have gotten Zeke so riled up.

"Can you believe these people?"

"What people?" Gloria was almost trembling – she had never seen Zeke so perturbed before in her life.

"These people have purposely deleted everything about when and how to merge from the state's driving laws. We live in a state where no one knows how to merge, and it's not even their faults!"

"Who? What people?" Gloria was confused.

"Oh, it must have been Director Langhorn. The director

of the Highways department back in 1959. That's when they would have deleted the requirements for merging in drivers' Ed."

"This is incredible, Zeke. What can you do about it?"

"We're gonna need to get a hold of a congressman to get this thing reinstated."

"Who are you going to talk to?"

"I think Congresswoman Phyllis Headache. She's fairly progressive and would be willing to listen . . . I hope."

Both Gloria and Zeke sat quietly, mystified that something like this could happen. Gloria rested her hand on top of Zeke's and stroked it softly to provide what comfort she could at such horrifying news. Minnesota was a state where any regard to merging had been thrown out the window. It was like the Wild West all over again – chaos and disorder was the law of the land.

Zeke decided to go into the office a little early on Monday to get a head start to his game plan for getting the merging laws reinstated. He wanted to start by going over the video tapes he had been making to see what the results might be of his "little test."

When he opened the door to the office he was a little stunned. It looked like a bomb had hit the place – files and papers everywhere. He walked through the office puzzled at what could have happened. Did some kids break in to vandalize the place? Even his desk had been overturned with mementos and office equipment strewn everywhere. He then heard something or someone in the back room. Was the burglar still there, he wondered to himself as his heart started to pound.

"All right, whoever is back there you better come out?"

There was no reply other than what sounded like someone rustling around. Zeke slowly walked toward the back room. He picked up a desk lamp from the floor to use as a possible weapon as he tip-toed slowly. As he reached the back room he slowly poked his head in. To his surprise he found Malaysia struggling – she had been tied to a chair and gagged. Zeke raced over to her to untie her.

"Malaysia, what happened?" he cried, as he pulled off the scarf that was tied over her mouth.

"Some big gorilla grabbed me and pulled me back here!"

"Did you get a good look at him?"

"No, he was wearing a gorilla mask."

"You mean he was dressed up as a gorilla?"

"Yes, kinda weird huh?"

"What did he want?"

"I'm not sure. I came in early this morning to start putting together those reports you wanted. I was in the back room putting my lunch in the refrigerator, and when I came out he grabbed me. I tried to fight with him, using all of my defense techniques, but the guy was like a gorilla. I think he may have *been* a gorilla."

Zeke shook his head a little puzzled at the thought of a trained gorilla coming into the office and ransacking the place.

"Anyway, he tied me up and then he went into the front office where I heard him going through everything. It sounded like he was destroying the place, but I don't know what he wanted."

A look of horror immediately ran over Zeke's face. "The tapes," he muttered to himself. He ran over to the filing cabinet where he kept the tapes and found they were gone. Malaysia came running in to find him rubbing the back of his neck.

"They got them."

Malaysia began to rub his neck trying to console him.

"What are we going to do, Zeke?"

"I'm not sure, but I bet Waxhead knows where those tapes are."

"Zeke, I'm sorry."

Zeke looked into Malaysia's deep blue eyes. If they could be any bluer they would be like the sky. He could look into them all day long. He felt is heart pounding. Her face looked vulnerable and her pursed lips began to quiver slightly. He found himself putting his arm around her waist and pulling her toward him. As she allowed him to pull her, they continued to gaze into each other's eyes.

"I'm really . . . sorry." Malaysia said as she bit her lip.

Their two lips engaged in a passionate embrace. Zeke could taste the sweet aroma of pineapple or coconut, or some other exotic fruit on her lips and on her tongue. He held her as tight as he could possibly hold someone. Malaysia, as usual was wearing one of her floral tight-fitting dresses that allowed him to be able to feel every curve of her sensuous body.

He slowly pulled back to look into her eyes. Was this the woman he had been waiting for all of his life? But what about the woman who had been there for him for almost all of his life? What about Gloria? Why was this happening?

"I . . . I'm sorry Malaysia."

"Sorry for what?"

"I'm sorry, but I'm married. I can't . . . I can't do this."

She slowly pulled away and nodded her head.

"I understand, Zeke. I guess I was just feeling a little vulnerable with all that has happened. Let's just pretend this didn't happen."

He was silent and stunned. How could he pretend this never happened? But she was right. It was a mistake and he had to think of Gloria. Despite what the world said, despite what the average Joe would do, it would not be right to treat the woman who had committed herself to him for twenty-five years – to just throw that away on some emotions – the passion of the moment. He loved Malaysia and would do just about anything to be with her, but not at the expense of his marriage.

"Ah, Malaysia, I think you're right. We had just better pretend it never happened."

A sad look came across her face. Perhaps she was hoping that he would tell her that pretending it didn't happen would be wrong, and that they should give into their feelings. But Malaysia loved Zeke even more for his strength, which was exactly why she felt the way she did. If she was Zeke's wife she would want to know that he was not willing to throw it all away for a younger woman.

To his relief, Jimmy Tinzdale came barging into the room in his usual fashion.

"Alright, what's going on here?" Jimmy said, with a look of a seasoned sheriff, sporting sunglasses and a toothpick. Malaysia immediately backed away from Zeke and walked toward her desk.

"Nothing!" Zeke stammered. "Well, no, it was not nothing," he corrected himself. "Someone broke into the office and tied up Malaysia."

"Really, why?"

"I don't know why, you idiot! Some moron came in here looking for something." As he said that he decided that he wouldn't say too much. Giving away information might not be the best thing, especially in the presence of Jimmy Tinzdale.

Jimmy began to walk around the office inspecting the damage. He looked over at Malaysia and asked her if she were okay, to which she responded in the affirmative.

"Hmmm. This doesn't look so good. I hope they didn't take your videotape, Zeke?"

Zeke said nothing. He had not mentioned anything about the videotape to Jimmy previously. The comment was very suspicious.

After the excitement of the morning, Zeke finally found time to watch the video. Luckily, he had made a duplicate copy and kept it inside of a hollowed-out flower pot. Although he was making a monthly study, he wanted to pull the videos each week to get a feel for what was going on. As he watched the video he couldn't tell if the action was real, or if the Marx Brothers had produced it.

The video had three camera angles – one from ground level where cars could be seen entering from Shakopee onto Highway 169 as well as from Savage. Another camera had been mounted on a lamppost right above the ground level camera, and another one across the street also mounted on a lamppost. All three of them showed the same thing – an ongoing multitude of potential accidents happening. Cars were constantly swerving and careering out of control, trying to avoid a collision with other cars as they merged.

What was really interesting to Zeke was the glee that some people had on their faces when they would not let other cars merge into their lane. It was almost like an unconscious reaction. A car would put their turn indicator on, and 99 times out of 100 the car they would be merging in front would immediately accelerate. It was literally that percentage. As Zeke view the videotape there where 6,721 instances out of 6,789 potential mergers where the car behind started to accelerate. It was almost like a giant light bulb went off in Zeke's head.

"Minnesotans are territorial!' he exclaimed out loud.

Malaysia peered into the conference room wondering what he was doing.

Zeke now had a theory about Minnesota drivers. As taxpayers for the roads, it was each Minnesotans right to own their own piece of the road. That piece of the road was like a small halo around the car that extended about ten feet all around them. No one was allowed within that halo or bubble. Anyone who violated that bubble would find quick retribution. It was all becoming clearer to him. And the biggest problem was, Minnesotans didn't even realize it – it was all in their subconscious – caused by years of never learning to merge.

The other part to the whole puzzle was that although each Minnesotan considered their brethren Minnesotan as

"Minnesota Nice," they knew subconsciously that their "brother or sister" would never let them merge smoothly. An instinct from birth was that they knew they had to merge as soon as possible, otherwise their fellow Minnesotan would never let them in.

Now it was off to test his theory, and his first stop would be the local driving school in Burnsville.

Zeke pulled up to "Sanderson's Driving School" on River Run drive off of Highway 13 in Burnsville. He walked into the rather distinguished building not knowing what to expect. As he walked into the reception area he was greeted by a young girl who was seated at a desk made entirely of glass. Apart from the space-age desk, the rest of the décor seemed to match that of early 1950s industrial, with a slight hint of art deco here and there.

"Hello, sir, my name is Candy. How may I help you?"

"Ah thank you, Candy, my name is William . . . .ah . . ."

Zeke looked around for some fake name he could call himself. He looked over the shoulder of the receptionist and spotted a calendar.

"Sandersons . . . s . . . ah Sandersons!!!" He then rolled his eyes as he realized it was a calendar from the driving school.

"Wow, you have the same last name as our driving school," the receptionist said, practically giggling.

"Actually my last name is Sandersons with an s on the end. Anyway, I'm interested in using your school for my daughter this year."

"Great, what's your daughter's name?"

"Ah, it's . . . ah, it's ah Aphrodite. Yes, Aphrodite."

"Great, well I'm sure Aphrodite will love it here. Can I get you to fill out this card, and then I will introduce you to Mr. Cornwall."

Zeke filled out the card which only required the most basic of information. He quickly slipped it back to Candy, who in turn made a call to Mr. Cornwall.

"Ah, Mr. Cornwall, I have a Mr. Sandersons here to see you. Yes Sandersons with an s on the end." The receptionist began to giggle incessantly. Zeke looked at her and tried to determine if her amusement was at his expense or at something Mr. Cornwall was saying to her.

He walked around the reception area, peering at the photos on the wall. It was like a wall of fame with what was probably Mr. Cornwall shaking hands with every student while presenting them with a sappy, oversized certificate of completion. The other thing he noticed was that there were pictures of Cornwall with Director Waxhead and ABC Towing president Harry Steel. In addition to those photos there was another picture that caught his eye – it was at a Christmas party with Cornwall holding a drink in one hand and shaking the hands of Sanderson Windows president John Pane. Actually there were all kinds of mementos, plaques and signage that showed that the driving school was owned by Sanderson Windows. But why would Sanderson Windows own a driving school?

As Mr. Cornwall walked into the reception area, Zeke could see that it was apparently only he that supervised the driving. Every picture was of him. Mr. Cornwall was quite portly with a broad mustache, and a nicely quaffed, greased-back head of black hair. He wore a stylish dress pants and shirt with tie and a sleeve-less sweater. He was quite posh, and Zeke was only waiting for him to break out the pipe.

"Mr. Sandersons I assume?"

"Yes, that be me."

"Very good. And who shall we be providing our services to Mr. Sandersons?"

"That would be my daughter."

"I see. And her name?"

Zeke stared at Candy trying to remember the name he had come up with. He started to make a twisting mouth movement hoping that some physical motion from his tongue would form the name he came up with. "Ah, it is . . . I mean to say, the name of my daughter is . . . ah."

Both Candy and Mr. Cornwall began to nod their heads in unison also trying to mouth the words Zeke was saying, and by doing so hope to try and draw out the name. Finally it came to Zeke.

"It's Aphrodite!!!"

"I see. Candy, let's start checking the appointment book for a free time for Aphrodite Sandersons."

As Cornwall, in his posh tone, repeated the name Zeke had come up with for his fake daughter, Zeke began to feel like he was three inches tall. Aphrodite Sandersons! His pet terrier could come up with a better name than that.

"Ah, well, before we make an appointment, Mr. Cornwall, I'd like to learn a little bit about your school if I may."

"Certainly, sir. It would be a pleasure. Why don't we have seat in my office?"

Mr. Cornwall motioned for Zeke to walk toward the back of the reception area where there was a hallway. Zeke walked hesitantly, unsure where he was going. The hallway seemed massive, with multiple doors to choose from. Mr. Cornwall quickly walked ahead of Zeke, noting his confusion on where to walk.

"Right this way, Mr. Sandersons, and just to your right there."

Zeke walked into Phil Cornwall's office and was greeted with an endless array of more congratulatory mounted photos, with Phil again extending a hand to another happy graduate.

"Ah, admiring my pictures, Mr. Sandersons?" Phil said, with a salesman's chuckle.

"It looks like you have had your share of satisfied students Mr. Cornwall."

"Please call me Phil," Cornwall said, as he offered Zeke a chair to sit.

"And may I call you by your first name, Mr. Sandersons?"

Zeke paused to try and come up with another name, but was drawing a blank.

"Why, sure. Now can you tell me a little bit about your school?"

"Sure, ah . . . ?" Phil was clearly fishing for Zeke's or "Mr. Sandersons'" first name.

Zeke, somewhat in a panic and completely forgetting he had just told the receptionist his name was William, looked down at Phil's desk and noticed a paper that looked like an invoice with a name on it . . ."Sandy Patrick."

"Ah, Sandy."

"Sandy?" Cornwall said a little puzzled. "Hmm, Sandy Sandersons?" Cornwall mused, at this lyrical name.

"Yes, ah, Sandy Sandersons."

"And a very nice name it is – a nice unisex name isn't it? Well, Sandy, here at Sanderson's Driving School we will put Aphrodite through an exhaustive battery of tests and will make sure she not only is a knowledgeable driver aware of all the driving laws, but also a safe driver."

As Zeke listened to Cornwall, his eyes dropped to the desk where he had spotted the invoice. He looked a little more closely and became horrified – it was an invoice from ABC Towing.

"You see, Sandy, here at Phil's we have a ninety-nine percent graduation rate, and we take great pride in our success. Our instructors have over ten years experience on average. They are personal and friendly and will make Aphrodite feel welcome and relaxed as she begins her lessons."

"Phil, that's really good to hear. So you will teach all of the basics, then?"

"Oh yes. We take them through their paces and start off slowly, teaching them how to park, parallel and otherwise. We show them how to move slowly out into traffic and how to . . ."

"Merge?" Zeke asked smugly.

Cornwall looked taken aback. He raised his eyebrows and took a deep breath. He paused for a moment and then spoke. "Oh sure. Absolutely we teach them to merge . . . I mean, of course, why wouldn't we teach them to merge? I mean we don't rush merging. I mean, that can be a difficult concept and we want to make sure our students are grasping the essentials first . . . Know what I mean?" Cornwall said with a wink.

"Oh sure, I know exactly what you mean," Zeke said with a nod.

Zeke asked Cornwall if he could meet one of their instructors, and he immediately ushered him out the office, clearly thankful that Zeke didn't have any more questions about merging. Cornwall showed Zeke to an office next door to his. As Zeke entered the office he was greeted by a beautiful young woman.

"Dorothy, I'd like you to meet Sandy Sandersons."

Dorothy extended a hand to Zeke which made him a little nervous.

"Yes, please call me Zeke," Zeke said with wet palm extended.

"Zeke?" she said, completely puzzled.

"Ah that's Z-Z-Z-Z-S-S-Sandy, I mean. Sorry, I get a little confused sometimes."

"Yes, anyway, Sandy has some questions for you, Dorothy." With that Cornwall left the room, his head shaking from the encounter.

"Can I get you a cup of coffee, Sandy?" Dorothy said, biting her lip – a lip that had been covered with some sort of lip gloss that made it glisten in the sunlight hitting the office.

"Ah no, that's fine."

"So how can I help you?"

"Well, I was noticing the other day that when I put my

blinker on to merge into another lane, a car immediately accelerated that was already in the lane I was signaling to change to. Clearly there are some issues with some drivers on how to correctly merge. Will you be teaching Audrey how to merge correctly?"

"Audrey?"

Zeke froze and tried to think of the fake name he had chosen for his fake daughter.

"What am I thinking . . . Audrey! I mean Allison! Phew, what's that all about?" Zeke said, in mock shame as he shook his head. He noticed Dorothy's smile turn to an almost pale look as if she were about to faint. He asked the question again and received an incoherent answer.

"Well, Sandy, we really try to focus on students maintaining a good speed, and for them to try and not move around too much – it can be a bit too much when we introduce the idea of trying to go sideways and perpendicular. We save merging for much later."

With that, Zeke requested that Dorothy take him to the parking lot in the back of the driving school where they would perform most of their maneuvers. He asked Dorothy to show him her merging technique. It was a terrible sight as Dorothy bumped the training vehicle into numerous other cars creating incredible damage and cost to the school. He knew there was a problem in Minnesota.

That night, he went home and began to write up proposals to the Department of Transportation. He even began to draft what he thought would be a good transportation bill, one he would call the "Minnesota Merging Act." He worked well into the night knowing the work he was doing could save the entire state of Minnesota. Then he turned on the Monster Truck rally on TV.

CHAPTER 7

A month later, Phil Speakeasy from Director Waxhead's office came barreling into the Burnsville office.

"Alright, Martin, we got your incident report and your complaint about merging and the road conditions. I'm sure the ransacking of your office was just some hoodlums . . ."

"What are you talking about, Speakeasy?"

Speakeasy turned to Zeke with a sharp stare.

"You've read my report, Speakeasy? Tell me what it says."

Speakeasy knew exactly what Zeke was talking about. The report that Zeke had worked on for over a month was compelling. It detailed a complete slackness for protocol within the department, no accountability to superiors, poor analysis and reporting on projects and potential projects. In summation, Zeke had an utter and complete pronouncement of failure for the department. The biggest failure cited was the complete and utter lack of ingenuity and planning for the 169 and 494 interchange. This had led to the suffocation of traffic coming from the southern suburbs. Those suburbs were the fastest growing in the entire state, and planning for the new inbound traffic from the south had been abysmal. Zeke had detailed how tempers had come to a boiling point with vehicle operators having to wait forty-five minutes just to get from the bridge to the 494. Road rage was not uncommon. People would run each other off the road and fights would break out. Drivers swerving at other drivers became commonplace. Rudeness and mean glares were also on an all time high. Eight out of ten drivers were now "giving rude looks" toward fellow vehicle drivers, cited one report from the Department of Driver Environment Research.

One of Zeke's statements was not so easy to take. It claimed that there was a conflict of interest for one of the nearby projects that has been started near the 169 and the 494. He stated that congressman Bob Turnout had met several times with Project Director Debra Stevens-Blatter. Zeke claimed that funds had been diverted from the 169/494 project in favor of making a "luxury frontage" road in the nearby town of Edina. The frontage road had been lined with elegant medians, complete with gas lamps and red brick. The road projects had taken ten months and covered an area of approximately a mile and half. New curbs had been installed along with sidewalks. The road had been repaved and the lane dividers brightly painted. Exotic plants, bushes and trees had been imported from Borneo making the street have an English colonial appeal to it. All in all, the project had cost the department and state taxpayers $13.5 million dollars.

What made matters worse was that Turnout hardly lived there. When he wasn't in Washington making a buffoon of himself, he went to his town-home in Palm Beach. His mother did live there and was apparently the reason for such a make over in the nearby frontage road – which was of little use to 85 year old Adda Turnout who no longer drove, or left the house for that matter.

"Martin, do you realize what you're saying in this report?"

Zeke gave Speakeasy a look of contempt. Of course he realized what he was saying. He wrote the damn thing!

Speakeasy strolled confidently around the room, eying the ceiling and waiting for a meek response from Zeke. Unfortunately he tripped over a ruffle on the carpet and landed helpless on one side. He moaned in pain as Zeke watched nervously, unsure whether to lend a hand or pretend nothing had happened. Malaysia offered Speakeasy a hand.

"I'm okay, I'm okay. Let's just get that damned tassel taken care of!"

"It's a ruffle" Malaysia conjectured.

"Whatever it is, I want it removed!"

Malaysia sashayed passed Speakeasy and walked toward her desk. Zeke was momentarily distracted by Malaysia's pedestrian activities. She immediately opened a document on her PC and started flailing away on the keyboard. The document contained a myriad of items Speakeasy had ordered her to take care of in the office. She now added, "Tassel on the rug" as a new item of consideration. Of course budget concerns would dictate whether these items would be resolved. Malaysia had become resigned to some of this type of work. With budget cuts, her investigative work had declined. She still was happy, knowing that she would one day get her turn at real road investigations. She would have her opportunities and her chances at promotion. And besides, nothing was holding her back: no husband, no family, no boyfriend, she could go anywhere where there was an opening. Her marital status quickly brought her to tears.

Speakeasy stared at Malaysia, wondering what she was now weeping uncontrollably about.

Zeke began to see that the two needed some psychiatric attention, but wasn't sure on how he might accomplish that at the moment.

"And what about the attack on the office last month? Are you not going to investigate it further? Malaysia could have been seriously hurt!" Zeke bellowed.

Speakeasy walked slowly over to Malaysia and began to eye her up and down. "Malaysia looks find to me," he said, with a sinister grin.

"You're sick, Speakeasy! I'm talking to Waxhead about this. I'm also going to present my finding on the 169/454 problem, as well as my month-long study on the merging issue. Clearly there is some sort of conspiracy here."

Speakeasy stared at Zeke. He began to run his fingers over his chin and began to walk over to Zeke. "'Month-long study'? You mean your video?"

Zeke could see he had struck a chord. He just nodded his head quietly. Speakeasy must know that he still had a copy of the video, despite the fact that Speakeasy knew the whereabouts of the original.

"Look, Zeke . . . old buddy, this is Minnesota. We are farmers and not big city people like you, apparently. We grew up in the fields and farms of Minnesota and all of these big highways and freeways, well . . . there are in a sense all new to us. Now let us as native Minnesotans provide the type of training and legislation we feel necessary to make the roads safe. Remember the old saying 'Minnesota Nice'? Well Minnesota people are plain, simple folk who are nice to each other. They understand when there's a little delay in traffic or if someone cuts them off because maybe their driving and merging skills are not quite like their brethren in Los Angeles or New York – it all works out in the end. Now if you play your cards right and don't rock the boat, Mr. Waxhead tells me he can make a few calls and get you reassigned to a nice choice location – perhaps Florida? Maybe your home state of Alabama? Just be smart, Zeke – don't rock the boat."

With that Speakeasy patted Zeke on the shoulder and headed out the door.

Zeke stared at Speakeasy as he got into his car and sped away. He shook his head in amazement and knew he was getting himself into a great deal of trouble. He turned and then found Malaysia almost shaking, with her hand covering her mouth as if to stifle a cry.

"What's the matter, Malaysia?"

Malaysia was still trembling, and Zeke moved over to try and console her.

"It was him!" she half shrieked.

"Him what?"

"It was Speakeasy who broke in here and tied me up!"

"How do you know?"

"Although he was hard to understand under the gorilla suit, I know the tone of voice, the body movement. Before he left, he made the exact same gesture as he made to you – he patted me on the shoulder and said 'don't rock the boat'."

Zeke was stunned. How could the heads of the Transportation department be acting this way? Clearly they were concerned, and not only concerned. If something didn't change soon they might hurt someone or perhaps kill someone. It was at that point Zeke realized he needed to get some legal counsel, and so he called Chandra Prahnpratvinchalnuralpravin of Prahnpratvinchalnural-pravin, Smithsonian, Wilson and Partners. Prahnpratvinchalnuralpravin was a recent immigrant from Thailand who specialized in civil law. He had written a much heralded book that made the top sellers list, *No Ur Rights and Do Not Have Ur Destiny Speedboats Water*. Actually it was on the best sellers' list in Thailand and Laos, but had been translated rather poorly into English. The author then quickly followed that masterpiece with his next work which was entitled *Friend, Have I Got an Aquatic Pancake Shovel Couch for You!* This didn't sell quite so well, but well enough to help move some of his family to the United States. "Mr. P" as Zeke was soon referring to him as, spoke little English and frequently used his partner Fred Smithsonian to interpret for him – which was a shame, since Smithsonian spoke little Thai.

Within the hour of making a phone call to Mr. P, he and Fred Smithsonian were meeting with him at Froggy's in

Shakopee. Jimmy Tinzdale was getting quite snoopy as of late, and Zeke wanted to ensure some secrecy as he met with the lawyer.

As Zeke poured some cream into his coffee he could see Smithsonian and Mr. P walking through the front door of Froggy's – it had to be them as they were the only two wearing suits within a fifty mile radius. Mr. P was also quite easy to distinguish. He was short, a little stocky and wore a perpetual smile on his face. He patted people on their shoulder as he walked through the entryway – smiling and waving to patrons who had confused looks on their faces – wondering who this character was.

"Hi, Zeke? Fred Smithsonian and Chandra Prahnpratvinchalnuralpravin," an enthusiastic Smithsonian said, as he extended his hand to shake.

A confused Zeke offered his hand to each gentleman. "Wow, you pronounce that very well . . . I think."

"Yes, well, I'm a student of Southeast Asia. I've always been fascinated with the Thai and Lao cultures. Spent a whole two weeks in Bangkok one year on vacation."

Zeke feigned admiration for Smithsonian's credentials and began to sip on his coffee. Smithsonian began to question him as to why he thought he had a case against the state. Zeke provided some documents he had put together and explained the lack of communication of the state statutes on merging. He also explained that there was a conspiracy to cause accidents so that the local towing companies could profit.

He then shared his proposal for amending the state law which he referred to as "The Minnesota Merging Act." While

Zeke spoke, Mr. P nodded his head with a bright smile on his face – completely in the dark as to what was being said.

Eventually Smithsonian spoke in Thai, or something similar to it for Mr. P's benefit. Mr. P shook his head in agreement and began to speak in the very tonal language that made that part of the world very unique. Smithsonian nodded his head and explained to Zeke.

"Ah, Mr. Prahnv . . . Prah . . . ah Mr. P thinks you have a strong case. He thinks that if we can perhaps get some conversations on patio furniture sale . . . I mean conversations on tape . . . sorry I always get confused on that word that would really add to the case. Do you think you can get some confessions on tape?"

"I'll see what I can do . . . I, ah . . ." Zeke stopped as he could see Mr. P writing something on a napkin. He quickly finished and passed it over to Smithsonian.

"Ah, let's see. Ah, it says, if we could only find stockpiles of purple lemons we could make far we can . . . Oh, wait that's if we could find some people to interview we can throw them over cliffs . . . no, no . . . It says if we could find some people to interview from towing companies we could put them in microwave ovens. Hold on . . ." Smithsonian quickly pulled a pocket-sized Thai-English dictionary from his coat pocket and again attempted to translate.

"Okay, one more time. It says if we could find some people to interview from towing companies that would help as well."

Smithsonian practically jumped for joy as he finally deciphered the scribble on the napkin. Zeke was also impressed and nodded his head in agreement.

Smithsonian gave Zeke his email address and asked him to start sending him any files he had electronically. Zeke advised against that, not knowing what the department might have or not have access to. Zeke decided the best method would be to bring things over to their office and drop it off in their mail box anytime he had something new. This way he could avoid anyone discovering on his computer the evidence he was assembling.

The two men quickly excused themselves, with Mr. P offering Zeke a cold sweaty hand, while Smithsonian unintentionally called him a pig in Thai. The three agreed to meet in two weeks to see where they stood on the case, and again encourage Zeke to dig a little deeper to uncover any more evidence. The more they had, the better the case they could make.

As Zeke drove home he received a call on his cell phone. "Hello, Zeke Martin here."

"Hi, Zeke – Bill Partyton here . . . president of the United Towing Industries Local 141."

Zeke grunted something inaudible while the union leader continued with his introductions.

"Say, Zeke, I hear you are helping to introduce some legislation regarding merging. Some silly thing called the Minnesota Merging Act? Well, we here at the Local 141 would like to encourage you to reconsider your position on that."

Zeke was quiet, sensing what Partyton was doing. The big question for Zeke was how could Partyton know about the legislation he was working on – including the working title?

"Zeke . . . Zeke! Are you still there?"

"Yes, Mr. Partyton, I'm here."

"You see, Zeke, it's like this. We help a lot of hard-working Minnesota families. The towing industry provides Minnesotans with good paying jobs and great benefits, and we do not want to see some renegade who is not familiar with the Minnesota road structure just come along and in ignorance throw a wrench into the whole works, creating chaos and putting good jobs at risk . . . Do you hear what I'm saying, Zeke?"

"So let me see if I understand you, Mr. Partyton. We should continue to put Minnesotans at risk on the highways so we can provide good paying jobs?"

"Look, Martin, you may see yourself as some sort of hero and do-gooder, but here in Minnesota we have a way of life, and it's not going to change just because of some golden boy from Alabama who thinks he knows it all."

The line went dead as Partyton hung up.

Zeke shook his head in confusion, wondering how people like Partyton could get into a position of power like that.

CHAPTER 8

As with every year, the employees of the transportation department were obligated to go to the Annual Holiday Ball that Director Waxhead put on each year. Everyone would need to gather at Waxhead's St. Paul mansion and pretend to enjoy the "joy of the season" as Waxhead would often say.

This year was a costume theme, something that Zeke particularly deplored. As he got off work that day he greeted his wife with a kiss and a painful expression on his face.

"Okay, what costume do you have for me?"

"Ah, well it's very original. You're going as Sigmund Freud."

"What?" Zeke cried, trying to contain himself. "And how pray tell is anyone going to know I'm Sigmund Freud?"

"It's easy. I've made you an old flannel suit. I've also made you a beard out of cotton balls . . . and best of all, I found these granny glasses at a local thrift shop that look just like his."

Zeke rolled his eyes, wondering why he couldn't just go as a cowboy or an Indian – native or otherwise.

"Look, here's the clincher. You'll go around the party with a pad and pencil and you'll psychoanalyze everyone. It'll be perfect."

"Why couldn't I have married a non-intellectual?" Zeke seemed to say to the ceiling.

"Because you're smart and you didn't want some ordinary woman, right?"

"Right. But what or who are you going as?"

"I will be Gertrude Stein."

"Anything else I should know before I shower and get ready?"

"I want to you to say the following as you talk with people. 'I see, and when do you first start noticing these tendencies?'" Gloria said in a mock German accent.

"What?"

"That's something Freud would say during one of his sessions."

"Right, I'm off to the shower."

Zeke hurriedly rushed upstairs, knowing that Waxhead would reprimand him for not getting to the ball on time.

He didn't particularly care what Waxhead thought, it was just being called out in front of his peers that was sometimes difficult. And as far as he knew, Waxhead might be at the center of one of the biggest conspiracies the state had ever known – caring what he thought meant little to Zeke.

After a quick shower and shave and splashing on of his favorite Aqua-Vinyl aftershave, Zeke begrudgingly put on his Sigmund Freud outfit, and he and Gertrude Stein were quickly out the door.

Zeke raced over to Waxhead's mansion as fast as he could, weaving in and out of the six o'clock traffic that seemed to be backed up going northbound of the Mississippi bridge and into St. Paul.

Zeke loved St. Paul. He loved the cathedral that was mirrored after Christopher Wren's London version and the old capital building. Something about St. Paul made him think of the way the east coast might be. It was a beautiful evening, one that he much preferred not wasting on Waxhead and his ilk, but he knew his wife loved to get out of the house for occasions such as these.

After what seemed like three hours, Zeke brought his car to a halt amidst a cloud of obscenities he was shouting at the neighborhood for not having enough street parking available. It was going to be a hike for them to get to Waxhead's mansion, and it was Zeke's lack of punctuality that Gloria would lecture him on as they walked the twelve blocks back over to the house.

"If you had listened to me and arrived a half hour ago we wouldn't have had to park so far away."

"Yes I know, darling, but now we can have this nice chat as we make our way over to Waxhead's"

Gloria looked over at him like he had been struck on the head with an errant brick. "Okay, what do you want to chat about?"

"Oh I don't know . . . the Magna Carter, the Louisiana Purchase . . . Perhaps Plato's arguments about a perfect plane . . ."

Just as the two began to step into the alleyway to cross the street, a burley African-American man stepped out of the shadows to block their path. "Hey, mister, got a minute?"

Zeke began to shake, and felt through his jacket to try and find his wallet.

"You might like some information I'm about to give you," the man said with a sinister grin.

"Ah, please, sir . . . I don't want any trouble." Zeke said, shaking even more, again fumbling around his jacket pockets for his wallet.

"Yah, I think you'll want to be in the know about this 411."

The man began to laugh with a strange howl. Both Zeke and Gloria trembled and turned white as ghosts. The man wore a plaid jacket with a bandana around his head, indicating he was in some sort of street gang.

"I'm sorry, I know it's here . . . Just give me a quick minute and I'll give you everything I've got."

When the man realized what Zeke was doing, an angry expression appeared on his face. "Man, I don't need your cracker money! I'm here to give you some information, Zeke Martin."

Zeke and Gloria were stunned.

"Do I know you?"

"Hell no. I work for the FBI. My name is Stephen Gerrard. Harvard educated and financially independent, thank you!"

"Oh Geez, I'm sorry. It's just your appearance is . . . is ah . . ."

"Yah, I'm working undercover. The Feds want an investigation of this whole merging thing and we're right behind you. Look, not a lot of time to give you the total info, but we have a man on the inside. You'll meet him tonight. He'll be going by the name of Trey Devin. Contact him and he'll give you further info."

"Okay, how do I know him?"

"He'll be the only brother there – except for Simmons of course. Simmons is the only black man that would be caught at that place . . . Know what I mean?"

"Yah, I know what you mean – that place is not cool yo!" Zeke looked around wide-eyed, hoping no one would see his incredible bad gansta impression.

"Yes, well, anyway, that's more or less the reason." The agent rolled his eyes and quickly disappeared into the alleyway.

Zeke and Gloria looked at each other with somewhat sheepish and ashamed looks on their faces that they would automatically think that the agent was going to rob them. They were quiet for the rest of the eight block walk to Waxhead's.

As Zeke and Gloria arrived at the front door they were greeted by a butler who promptly took their coats.

"Mr. and Mrs. Zeke Martin," the butler called out to the guests assembled in the foyer.

The mansion was spectacular and Zeke, who had been there several times, could never get over its opulence. The entry way was lined with marble columns, with cherry teak wood on the walls carved into various scenes of the founding of Minnesota. It had been hand-carved in Laos and then exported to Minnesota where it was assembled. As he and Gloria walked into the foyer they stepped onto a beautiful floor made of Italian marble tiles, alternating between white and turquoise. On either side were elegant stairways leading to hallways on the second floor. Incredible antique gas lamps lined the walls of the foyer, giving it a look of a ballroom on the Titanic.

As they made their way through the foyer they were immediately intercepted by another butler who offered them a glass of champagne. The first thing that Zeke noticed at the ball was how Jonathan P. Farnington was continually in the ear of Waxhead. Zeke wasn't sure if he was fixated on the pair because of their chatting together, or on what they were wearing. Waxhead was wearing a Godzilla costume that was ridiculous. Farnington on the other hand was dressed as a scuba diver complete with oxygen tanks.

Zeke had his suspicions about Farnington, his family owning a wealthy towing company south of the river (Minnesota River that is). Zeke asked Gloria to mingle while he tried to find the FBI agent. He wandered down one of the halls toward his favorite place. Waxhead had a poolroom complete with wet bar and widescreen TVs all tuned into the latest pennant race, horse race or whatever finals happened to be on. In this case it was nearing the end of the football season, and the Multi-National Football League's Monday Night broadcast had the Green Bay Crackers (with Cheese) pitted against the Minnesota Norsemen. Zeke was not a big fan of the professional game and would try and bribe everyone to watch the annual classic between Coastal Alabama and Alabama Auto Tech. Every year that was the game he waited to see.

In one corner he noticed two African-American men watching basketball. The Minnesota Timber Cutters were taking on the Utah Classical Music.

"Can I interest you boys in a little Southern Division 5-AA football?" Zeke said, as he sauntered over to the two men, not seeing the Persian rug with one edge protruding heavenward as if imploring any walker-by to tempt its tripping power.

With one quick motion he was flat on his face, having become the carpets intended victim. The two men scrambled to help him off the floor.

"Zeke . . . ah, you okay?" Hezekiah Simmons offered. Simmons was the man the agent had referenced as being the only other "brother" at the party. Simmons, although disdaining the typical trappings of a party with mostly "white folk," understood the need for such things in order to get ahead. Many of his "brethren" would not go for such a thing, but Simmons felt it imperative if he was going to move up within the Department of Transportation.

"Oh, what an idiot I am!" Zeke exclaimed, as he jumped to his feet. "It's clear I've lost my athletic moves!" He laughed as he tried to imitate the Heisman trophy.

Both Simmons and the other man laughed, both wondering who or what Zeke was trying to impersonate.

"Hey, Zeke, I'd like you to meet Trey Devin."

"Ah, yes, Mr. Devin, it's good to meet you. I've heard so much about you."

"All good I hope?"

"Nothing but rave reviews. Say, I was wondering if I could have a quick word with you?"

"Ah sure, Hezekiah, we'll be right back."

The two men walked into a neighboring hallway that

looked somewhat private.

"Zeke, thanks for drawing so much attention to my presence here."

Zeke's face went beet-red, knowing that Devin was referring to his flop on the floor a few minutes earlier. "Yah, sorry about that."

"Oh, don't worry. Most every one here is drunk anyway, and they won't put two and two together."

Devin motioned for Zeke to walk further down the hall and away from potential interlopers.

"Anyway, I think you were approached by a gentleman in the alleyway earlier?"

Zeke nodded, trying to bury the embarrassment of the event in the back of his mind.

"What he was referring to is an operation that I think you yourself have been suspecting should be in place. The government thinks there's something fishy going on here in the beautiful state of Minnesota."

Zeke looked pensive and nodded, not wanting to let the agent think he had the entire inside information.

"Clearly something is happening with the rate of accidents here corresponding with the incredibly high revenues generated by the towing industry."

Again Zeke nodded, preferring to not let the agent know that he had made a similar connection.

"Zeke, we need someone like you on the inside."

"Me? Aren't *you* in the 'inside'"?

"Yes, well, sort of. I'm just an assistant in the federal office. Waxhead runs a close-knit group at the capital, and I haven't been able to crack that group or get a promotion there – even with Washington's help."

"So, what do you want me to do?"

"Just sniff around. You have access that many don't. What's more, they'll never suspect you. They think you're an outsider anyway – a guy from Alabama. These Minnesotans only trust themselves."

"Yah, that's true."

"I mean, have you ever been invited to a picnic or a barbeque in Minnesota?"

"Only ones that are sponsored by the department."

"Yah, that's what I mean. These people stick to themselves. They're either at their cabins up north or with one of the other twelve siblings they grew up with going over to their 'sister's' or 'brother's' house."

"Now that you mention it – that is always the excuse someone has if they can't do anything."

"Have you every noticed in the almost twenty years that you have lived here that you have never had a social event with either one of your neighbors?"

"Hmmm . . . How did you know that?"

"I don't have to know – you live in Minnesota! And they talk about 'Minnesota Nice' – its Minnesota Ice more like it!"

"Boy, you sure seem to know a lot about Minnesota?"

"Yah, I grew up here."

Zeke did a double-take almost worthy of 1960s television sitcom.

"Okay, so go and mingle. I need you to sniff around. Anything significant you find, just text me."

Zeke nodded and proceeded back into the party in the

main foyer. He quickly eyed the assembly and tried to see what he could find out. Near Waxhead was Ashton Vanderhilt, President of 4M (Minnesota Miming, Mimicry and Masquerade) a multi-billion dollar costume and production company. He was dressed as a swash-buckling pirate. On Waxhead's left was Bill Blatterton from General Silos, the multi-billion dollar grain and cereal company famous for their brands such as Wheatie-O's and Frosted Shredded Banana Nuts. He was dressed as a Siamese Twin with one fake head that exactly resembled his actual head.

As Zeke walked slowly toward the gathering of these "Captains of Industry" he confidently reached for a glass of champagne from the tray of a neighboring waiter, and sent it careening onto the floor in what seemed a million shards of glass. Zeke confidently motioned to a waiter to fetch a broom and wipe up the remnants. The waiter replied with his middle finger extended.

Zeke, ever the trooper, proceeded toward the group of assembled corporate giants.

"Ah, Zeke, how are you tonight?" Waxhead said, feigning interest. He turned to his companions. "Gentlemen, I'd like you to meet Zeke Martin. He runs our branch south of the river here – Zeke does fine work. Currently finishing up on that bit of bad business we had in Shakopee."

The men smiled and extended their hands to Zeke.

"That must be exciting to work on such an investigation Mr. Martin?" said Walt Kaisersummer, CEO of Betty Crockpot, a subsidiary of General Spills (the floor wax and other household cleaning products conglomerate), a subsidiary of General Silos, and dressed as Sir Isaac Newton.

"Call me Zeke. Ah yes, very exciting indeed. But I imagine your line of work is quite exciting as well?"

"Sure is. We're right in the middle of preparing our financial statements and it's *very* exciting. There is nothing like this time of the year where I preside over a sea of accountants to prepare our financial statements."

Zeke nodded and began to search around for a waiter carrying anything alcoholic.

"You see, Mr. Martin . . . I mean, Zeke. What's fascinating is that although we are a subsidiary of General Spills and a further subsidiary of General Silos, we have to prepare our own financial statements . . ."

Zeke nodded his head like some sort of possessed puppet, all the while trying to keep an eye on Waxhead who was now chatting with Vanderhilt.

." . . . You see, GAO accounting regulations require that we report inventory as FIFO, and thus it is important that we stay on top of our inventory and ensure that we accurately report all sales and inventory in clear and precise terms . . ."

Zeke began to fantasize that he was a French soldier in Napoleon's army retreating from Moscow in the dead of winter.

" . . . GAO to me, Zeke, should be renamed to the General Agony Office, if you get my drift . . ."

Zeke's mind was now drifting away, imagining various car crashes and ships sinking from various adventure and horror movies he had seen.

"Umm, this is very interesting, Mr. Kaisersummer, but I think I better mingle a bit. Bye!"

Zeke began to walk around the gathering and quickly spotted Devin in the crowd. Devin stared at Zeke as if waiting for some sort of message from him. Zeke shook his head letting Devin know he had not been successful.

"Ladies and gentlemen, I would like you to adjourn to the next room – which Mrs. Waxhead and I like to refer to as the Wisconsin Room. There we will be entertained by the Budapest Boys' Choir."

The crowd slowly flowed into the Wisconsin Room in a more orderly fashion than any lane-change on a Minnesota highway. True to the name Waxhead had given to the immense room, the walls were adorned with paintings and various artifacts found in the wilds of Wisconsin. At the center of the room was an enormous Norway pine that towered to the glass roof of the room. Around the base of the tree was the Budapest Boys' Choir already in full form, belting out a traditional Yuletide song.

Zeke found Gloria and offered her his arm as they made their way through the impressive doorway. He offered Gloria some punch from a table that was stationed on the right side of the choir. On the left side of the choir was a stairway that led to a second level from where many of the partygoers were using to look down upon the choir. After offering Gloria her punch, Zeke mentioned that he should mingle a little more and that he was planning to go up to the second level.

Once he arrived at the top, he spotted Bill Partyton, the Towing Union President or what he thought was Partyton – he resembled Pancho Via. Zeke sauntered slowly up behind Partyton as to not disclose his presence. Partyton was talking with a union rep and Zeke did not want to disturb their conversation.

With Partyton's back turned to Zeke, Zeke placed his hands on the railing, looking down to the scene below. The union rep did not know him, so he felt assured he could linger there without being suspected or detected by Partyton. Zeke sipped his punch and leaned his head toward the conversation. He could hear bits and pieces as the two men whispered, but he needed something else that might magnify what was being said. From his jacket pocket he pulled out his iBlueberryPodPort – his mobile phone, music player and voice recorder. As he pulled it out, he put his earplugs in to give the appearance he was listening to tunes, but all the while was actually listening to the conversation.

As the two men talked, Zeke slowly moved the iBlueberryPodPort toward them. He listened intently . . .

"You see, Mike, with this new contract we will be able to double our pay for each hour of overtime worked, but it is imperative that we work closely with Waxhead on this. There are some rumblings that people want to change traffic laws. Any changes could spell disaster for our way of life . . ."

Zeke could not believe what he was hearing, and to ensure he was getting every word he could, he moved the iBlueberryPodPort closer. But as he did, Partyton, trying to emphasize a point, swung his arm back knocking the iBlueberryPodPort out of Zeke's hand.

Zeke tried to grasp at the electronic device and was almost successful. He managed to nick it with his fingers causing the iBlueberryPodPort to pop up into the air over the railing. He leaned over the railing trying again to grasp at it like it was a fumbled football during his college years. He again bobbled the device as it came near him, but he again accidentally batted it away. He lurched forward but fell over the railing and onto of the great Norway pine that had been decorated so immaculately.

The assembled crowd on the bottom floor turned and looked in horror as Zeke began to tumble down the Christmas tree, spraying the assembly below with assorted lights and decorations. He seemed to bounce from branch to branch like some sort of pinball game, causing even the boys' choir to look on in rapt awe, still hitting every note of Ave Maria.

As Zeke hit the bottom branch, it seemed to cradle him and then gently raise him to his feet as if the entire fall had been choreographed. He stepped off the helpful branch right in the back row of the choir. Trying not to be noticed, he immediately began to mouth the words to "God Rest Ye Gentle Merry Men."

Although Zeke's sudden arrival had placed him perfectly between two of the choir members, it was painfully obvious that being a foot taller than the boys on either side of him he was clearly not a member of the choir. Yet, like the trooper he was, Zeke was not going to spoil the show. He continued to mime and gesticulate until the final crescendo.

As the music came to an abrupt end, the entire assembly began to clap wildly with applause, guessing that the plunge had been orchestrated to correspond with the choir.

"That was terrific, just terrific!" Mr. Lipbalm, CEO of Piper Joffery Laurie Investments screamed with enthusiasm while dressed as Christopher Wren.

"Wonderful, just wonderful!" applauded a nearby Steve Westingtonson, Executive Vice President at Northbest Airlines, dressed as the Mad Hatter.

Zeke brushed himself off and, looking up, could hardly believe the applause he was receiving. He took a quick bow and then tried to blend his way back into the crowd.

"That was tremendous!" Phil Cranburg, Chairman of EhoesLab and dressed as a grizzly bear crowed as he grabbed Zeke by the arm. "However did you learn to do that?"

"Ah, lots of practice," Zeke said shyly, trying to see who was talking through the large jowls of the bear.

As the applause subsided, Zeke weaved his way toward a target he had been eying for most of the evening – it was Waxhead himself.

"Zeke, tremendous job tonight – I think I'm going to have to put you in charge of next year's entertainment, ha, ha, ha, ha, ha, ha, ha, ha . . . ha."

Zeke was baffled by the "ha-ha-ha's," but secretly moved his hand inside his jacket pocket to turn on the iBlueberryPodPort he had retrieved from a nearby punchbowl.

He took a quick moment to regain his composure and grab a cup of the Christmas punch. Philip Coldcut, CEO for Medtonic, joined him. As Coldcut began to babble on about a similar fall he had taken during a Christmas several years prior, Zeke noticed Jimmy Tinzdale talking with the mayor of Shakopee. Jimmy was sporting a cowboy outfit complete with guns and holsters – Zeke just prayed they were not real. With Jimmy anything was possible.

"It was amazing! I was about to place the star on the top of the tree when the next thing I know I'm tumbling down the tree and whacking my head on the floor! It was hysterical!"

Zeke look closely at Coldcut and could see why profits at Medtonic had been declining over the past couple of years.

"Boy, you don't see that every day!" Coldcut quipped.

Zeke looked over to where Coldcut was nodding. Joining Jimmy and the mayor of Shakopee was John Pane, the CEO of Sanderson Windows. Zeke asked Coldcut why it was so unusual. Coldcut hesitated but decided to speak. He explained that a year earlier Jimmy had run for mayor of Shakopee against Fred Zwindler. He also surprisingly mentioned that Pane had helped Jimmy with financing of his campaign. It was only because of Jimmy's ineptitude that he lost the race.

As Coldcut related the story, it was clear that something was afoot in the race, so-to-speak. When Zwindler gained an early lead in the election, the Tinzdale campaign quickly put out smear ads on local television. The problem with local TV was that the ads had no impact on the largely rural folk of Scott County. Jimmy next tried to bribe the community by offering free towing for one month. But it was the debate between Jimmy and Zwindler that really did in the campaign.

The debate started off decent enough with both candidates making adequate opening remarks, but it soon descended into a frenzy of obscenities and insults – and that was just from the moderator! But it was Jimmy's youth and lack of experience that would soon do him in.

At one point Jimmy referred to Shakopee as Savage, the neighboring town, as he was a resident of Savage. He also made brash promises that clearly the townspeople of Shakopee did not believe, like "Free-Fridays" where everything in town would be free, no income, state or property taxes, 75% discount on all utilities and finally a guarantee that Shakopee (which he again referred to as Savage), would never come under the rule of foreign invaders such as the Soviet Union. It was clear Jimmy had no clue what he was talking about, and so it was a landslide in Zwindler's favor. What Coldcut whispered to Zeke at the end was even more amazing. There were rumors that Waxhead had wanted Jimmy to become mayor of Shakopee because Zwindler was trying to raise corporate taxes – a move that Shakopee-based ABC Towing was none too pleased about.

As Zeke listened to Coldcut, it was becoming abundantly clear what was happening, and Zeke now knew why Jimmy had been assigned to his office. Zeke decided to keep an eye on Jimmy throughout the evening and see whom he might come in contact with. After noting some interesting encounters Jimmy had with the heads of Malibou Coffee and Mole-D-Meal, Zeke decided to track Jimmy Tinzdale down in the one of the hallways.

"Hey, Jimmy, having a good time at your uncle's party?"

Jimmy, a little ways down the hall, tried to ignore Zeke at first. He was chatting with a young woman. Zeke walked toward the pair and extended his hand to Jimmy to shake. Zeke pulled back his hand, now sweat-soaked from Jimmy's perspiring palms and began to wring them out like he had just washed them in the sink.

"Sorry, it's a little hot in here," Jimmy said, trying to look confident in front of the woman.

"And so, remember to always use mercantile fidelity when planning any fiduciary funding and stock enhancements to your portfolio, Kim."

Kim shook her head, smiling, but not having a clue what Jimmy was talking about.

"Sorry, Zeke, I was just trying to impart some financial wisdom to my friend Kim here."

"But aren't you supposed to always sell high and buy low?" a perplexed Kim said, apparently remembering the remnants of an earlier conversation.

"Well, enough of that. Say, Kim, how 'bout some punch?"

A confused Kim, dressed as what appeared to be a swan but what Zeke thought made her look like a cheap prostitute, wandered off alone, looking for the aforementioned punchbowl.

"Great party, eh, Zeke? By the way, who are you supposed to be?"

"Sigmund Freud."

"Oh you mean the racecar driver?" Jimmy said, completely ignoring the fact that Zeke was wearing fake glasses, a fake goatee and mustache, a grey wig and carrying a pipe.

"Yes, that's exactly who I am. And you are right, it is a great party, Jimmy, and I couldn't help but notice how well you work the crowd."

"I do?"

"Well, yes. You were hobnobbing with some of the biggest movers and shakers in town. I don't see you staying long in our little neck of the woods."

Zeke laughed and elbowed Jimmy in the arm, giving him a wink of the eye. Jimmy rubbed his arm and laughed a confused laugh, wondering what Zeke was implying.

"Why is it you work for us, Jimmy?"

Jimmy shook his head and slowly began to walk down the hallway trying to make his escape.

"I mean, the nephew of such a powerful man in the state government – clearly you could be doing better than working in a field office for the department of transportation in Shakopee, Minnesota?"

Jimmy started to quicken his pace. "I like what I do," he said rather unconvincingly.

"Yah, I mean all the action we have – it must be thrilling for you?"

"Look, Zeke, what are you getting at?"

"Oh nothing. Just wondering out loud why you're assigned to my office. Is there another reason I should know about?" Zeke decided he would go all the way with his inquiry and start getting things out in the open. "You wouldn't be spying on us would you?"

"Spying on you? That's preposterous! Absurd!"

Zeke silently stared at Jimmy, hoping his pointed gaze might break him.

"You're crazy, Zeke. I'm just trying to break into the department. My superiors felt this would be a good opportunity to get my feet wet."

Again Zeke held his gaze, not batting an eye. He just let

Jimmy keep talking.

"I mean c'mon, what else would I be doing, huh?" Jimmy said, in a mocked huff and raised shoulders. "I'm not doing anything – I mean why would I be spying?"

And then Jimmy said something that shocked Zeke. It was something actually unexpected and intelligent. "I mean, what would I be looking for? Is there some reason I should be spying?"

Zeke was surprised Jimmy could come up with such a good come-back. Zeke remained calm and just shrugged his shoulders. Jimmy smiled, knowing that he had turned the tables. It was something he seldom accomplished and the smug smile on his face betrayed his self-satisfaction. He then turned triumphantly and walked back into the main ballroom as if he had just won an eighteenth century duel. His rapier wit would be seldom displayed again.

Zeke smiled as he watched the pompous Mr. Tinzdale strut down the hall. Although Jimmy didn't admit to anything, Zeke had all the information he needed, through studying Jimmy's defensive body-language. Things were starting to add up and it was clear he would need to get things moving with Mr. P.

"Ah, Director Waxhead, may I have a word with you in private?"

"After that performance, anything, my boy!"

Zeke slowly ushered Waxhead to a secluded area near the bar"

"How's that deer reduction program going, Zeke?"

"Well, not so good . . . I hit another one last night."

"Oh, I see."

"Anyway, DIRECTOR WAXHEAD . . ." Zeke said loudly, with overly articulated syllables that made him look like he was trying to do jaw exercises. Director Waxhead looked at him like he was having a seizure.

"DIRECTOR WAXHEAD, I WAS TALKING WITH JOHNNY ZANZIBAR OF XYZ TOWING YESTERDAY, AND HE WAS SAYING THAT IF IT WASN'T FOR HAROLD P. WAXHEAD'S GENOROSITY HE WOULD NEVER BE ABLE TO MAKE SUCH A GOOD LIVING. WHAT DO YOU HAVE TO SAY TO THAT, MR. WAXHEAD?"

Director Waxhead looked slightly uncomfortable as Zeke lifted and pointed his left shoulder practically into his chest. Now he was really convinced that Zeke was having a seizure. Waxhead raised his hand to signal to Zeke to keep his voice down. He began to look down either side of the hall. Zeke followed his lead and they looked like two spectators at a tennis tournament.

"Ah, let's go into my study for a moment Zeke."

"OKAY, DIRECTOR . . . LET US GO INTO YOUR STUDY TO TALK . . . TALK CANDIDLY."

One thing Zeke would never be accused of was being a good actor. A good musician maybe, but his acting skills left a lot to be desired.

As they arrived at the huge oak door of Waxhead's study, Zeke was taken aback by the huge deer head that was placed on the door. It not only seemed like a strange place to hang a deer head but it made it almost impossible to get inside, having to negotiate around the large antlers. As Zeke slid into the study he came eyeball to eyeball with the great buck. He began to feel guilty for all of the deer he had hit in the past.

"Shot 'im on a hunting trip in '03. Biggest kill of my life. Huge beast isn't he?"

Zeke nodded his head in agreement.

"That buck represents me, Zeke. When I go after something I go after it whole hog . . . I don't do things half way. Likewise if something gets in my way I don't hesitate to eliminate that threat . . . Know what I mean, Zeke?" Waxhead was staring directly at Zeke, and it was hard to miss the point he was making.

"Anyway, you said you spoke with Johnny Zanzibar?"

Zeke again nodded silently in agreement.

"Great guy Zanzibar. He came to this country in 1994 with nothing but a few dollars in his pocket. He came from an impoverished nation . . . Ah, what was the name . . . ?"

"Zanzibar?"

"No, it was one of the 'Stans. Pakistan, Uzbekistan, Trifectastan, I can't remember. Anyway, Johnny was a taxi driver at the airport and he saved his money up so he could buy a tow truck. After a couple of years he started to make some money so he bought himself a garage and a couple more tow trucks. He brought his family over from the 'Stan and he began to do well. After another year or so though things went a little stagnant for him and he came to me for a loan. I obliged and decided that Johnny and his family would be a good investment, and so I loaned him $5,000. That was the best investment I ever made. Johnny has since paid me back threefold. Not a bad deal, eh?"

"Ah yes, Director, a very good deal, but was there anything ELSE THAT HAPPENED? DID YOU MAKE

THINGS EASIER FOR JOHNNY?"

"Whatever do you mean, Martin? And can you stop talking so loudly and so slowly?"

"OH SORRY, DIRECTOR I WILL TRY AND DO THAT. BUT . . . but what I mean is some of the boys in the department have been talking that you make things easier for some businesses."

"Look, Zeke, I'm a businessman at heart. I run this department like a business, not like a lot of those bureaucrats in Washington. That's why this department is efficient and that's why you've been able to climb the government grading system so quickly."

Waxhead walked over to Zeke and put his arm around his shoulder.

"Look, Zeke, you're not from these parts. Minnesotans have always looked out for each other, and when a business opportunity comes up we like to help each other out. Now you are from Alabama, right? Look at all the time you've been here and you still don't act like a Minnesotan. You'll never be a Minnesotan, because you don't fit in."

"And Johnny Zanzibar does?" Zeke said, with a puzzled expression.

"Ah well, yes, Johnny comes from one of the Northern most 'Stans that is very similar to Norway, which is what most Minnesotan's heritage is. Johnny grew up just a little further east of Norway."

"Yah, right next door in Mecca. He's actually from Saudi Arabia."

"Really?" Waxhead said, with genuine confusion on his face. "See! See how open-minded us Minnesotan's are? It's you outsiders who don't understand this. We have always opened our arms to aspiring business people regardless of race, creed, religion, etc., etc."

"I see, so you don't think the environment here in Minnesota is unsafe though? I mean, why do we need so many tow truck companies?"

"It's simple, Zeke. We have a lot of accidents here in Minnesota – plain and simple, we drive like farmers in the big city. I mean, that's what you want to hear. Right, Zeke? All of us hicks from the Northern Plains don't know how to drive. Right, Zeke? Our roads not good enough for you. Right, Zeke?"

Waxhead began pointing his finger into Zeke's chest, which was exactly what he wanted. He hoped his iBlueberryPodPort was picking up everything, despite the Tahitian punch bath it had just recently been through.

"You're probably just like that Mallard guy that came from California. You think we're a bunch of crazy idiots on the roads, hey, Zeke?"

Zeke was puzzled that Waxhead could throw Mallard's name around so easily. Sure his name was mentioned in the papers a time or two, but unless he had been following his investigation closely it would be hard to remember such a thing.

"Director, all I'm trying to figure out is why our accident rate is so much higher than the average state. I'm just trying to help save lives."

"Look, Zeke, that's why I want you working fulltime on this deer thing. I think you will find that there is an easy explanation to our accident rate – it's the deer. We are a land of hunters and fishermen. We drive in rural places and we run into deer a lot . . ."

"But the evidence would suggest that those are only a small fraction of the accidents . . ."

"Have you done any formal research? You yourself have hit half a herd of those damn things, haven't you?"

"Well . . . ah, yah, but . . ."

"But nothing. I want you to start working on that report on deer strikes. I want this research to last two years. I want you to analyze the heck out of it. I want to know everything you can find out about deer strikes. I may even create a separate department for you, with you heading up the whole project. What do you thing about that, Zeke?" the Director said, as he stretched out his hand like he was trying to weave a panorama or vision of such a department.

Zeke sighed, trying to imagine spending his fulltime trying to analyze the one creature that was giving him nightmares every night.

"Managing Director of Deer and Road Management. This would be an important promotion, Zeke. What do you think? You would report directly to me. You could have every other weekend at my cabin, access to a government car." Waxhead began to look around again, like the tennis match was back on.

"I'll even give you two weeks a year at our condo in Hawaii."

"Ah, thank you, Director Waxhead, but I'll need to think about it."

"You do that, Zeke, you do that."

Waxhead patted Zeke on the shoulder and then reached

out his hand to shake. Zeke reluctantly reached out his hand and reciprocated. He slowly walked out of the study, somewhat in shock, somewhat in haze about what to do.

Zeke bid Waxhead a quick farewell and then tried to find Gloria. On the way over to the Wisconsin room to find her he spotted Trey Devin, and they immediately made eye contact. Devin nodded to Zeke, which was his signal to drop anything to him that he might need. As Zeke walked over to him he slowly removed the iBlueberryPodPort from his jacket pocket and stealthily slipped it into Devin's hands . . . or so he thought. He actually missed Devin's hands and the device bounced onto the floor with a loud crash that made half of the partygoers turn and look. Zeke smiled and then tried to not look suspicious.

"EXCUSE ME, SIR, YOU MUST HAVE DROPPED YOUR iBLUEBERRYPODPORT AS I DO NOT OWN ONE. HERE, PLEASE ALLOW ME TO PICK IT UP AND HAND IT TO YOU," Zeke said, with a bizarre forced smile on his face as agent Devin rolled his eyes. Zeke reached out to shake Devin's hand thinking that it would look like Devin, the lucky recipient of his lost electronic device, was rewarding him for his act of kindness. Devin's expression turned to anger.

"Okay, you are only drawing more attention to yourself. Get lost!" Devin said, in a controlled whisper.

Zeke got the hint and quickly gathered Gloria to depart for home. Gloria was confused by Zeke's need to leave all of sudden, but hoped it might be for a good reason. On the walk back to the car Zeke grabbed her hand, and she looked at him with a rather surprised but happy expression.

"Well, you look like you had a busy night," Gloria remarked, as Zeke opened the car door for her.

"Yah, you wouldn't believe how busy."

But Gloria did know how busy, as she happily replayed the evening's events in her mind from the tripping over the Persian carpet to the fifty foot plunge down the Director's Christmas tree. Zeke seemed oblivious to Gloria's laughter as he pulled onto the main highway. As he drove onto the highway he immediately plowed into a herd of deer.

"Where do these damn things come from!!!?" he screamed into the December night.

Several weeks later a clandestine meeting took place at Director Waxhead's house in St. Paul. Assembled were Waxhead, Jimmy Tinzdale, Harry Steel and Sanderson Window's CEO, John Pane.

"Gentlemen, I've called you here because we need to discuss this Martin business."

Waxhead had the gentlemen seated around a large oaken round table. There were old tenth century English war banners hanging from the walls that made the room appear like something from Arthurian legend. Waxhead referred to it has his "war room." He motioned to a butler who was standing at attention by the door. The butler immediately poured four glasses of brandy and presented each guest with the liquor and a Cuban cigar from a silver tray.

An intercom device on the table began to ring. Waxhead stared at it with the air of a five-star general waiting for his call from the President to mobilize the troops. He casually pushed the button to the intercom.

"Harry, it's almost 7:30. Slip on your jammys and come watch Wheel of Fortune with me."

"Dear, I'm in an important meeting right now, so don't bother us!"

"But honey-bear, you always told me to tell you when the Wheel is on . . ."

Waxhead, perturbed, slapped at the switch to the intercom. "Gentlemen, my nephew Jimmy here has some valuable information about what's happening in our Burnsville office."

Jimmy stood up and walked over to a flip chart that he had written the name of Zeke Martin. Jimmy pulled out a pointer from a clip that housed an array of communication devices and other equipment he always kept near him.

"Gentlemen . . . honey-bear . . . ," Jimmy giggled to himself, with Steel and Pane also joining in. One look from his uncle however and his glee was turned to a more serious look. He proceeded to flip the chart and a strange image appeared that resembled the face of a man.

"Gentleman, this is our enemy." Jimmy pointed to a figure that looked like it had been scribbled with felt pen.

"Abraham Lincoln?" Harry Steel queried.

"No, not Abraham Lincoln! How does that look like Abraham Lincoln – it doesn't even have a beard?" quipped Director Waxhead.

"Well, it's clearly Adolph Hitler!" cried the Sanderson Windows CEO.

"How can that be Adolph Hitler?" Jimmy yelled in anger.

"Well he's got that thin mustache, right?"

"That's not a mustache. That's the . . . ah, the . . ."

"Philtrum, sir?" the butler chimed in.

"Yes, exactly James, the Piltrim."

"The P-H-I-L-T-R-U-M, sir."

The assembled gentlemen looked puzzled.

"The Philtrum. The Philtrum or *infranasal depression*, is the vertical groove in the upper lip formed where the nasomedial and maxilary processes meet during embryonic development."

Everyone stared long and hard at James the butler, impressed with his knowledge of facial anatomy. Jimmy continued.

"Gentlemen, this guy is probably worse than Hitler." Jimmy paused and rolled his eyes, silently acknowledging his blunder. "What I mean, he is probably worse than Hitler for our own personal lives . . . .ah, not in the whole scheme of world politics and history."

Despite Jimmy's effort to recover from his monumental guffaw, the White, Anglo-Saxon Protestants were hardly concerned for the allusion to the Aryan leader – they cared only for the money they could lose, and not the world at large.

"Anywho, this man Zeke Martin could unravel all that you gentlemen have built over the years. Zeke Martin is on a campaign to overhaul our driving regulations and to get people to merge correctly."

The men sighed in unison, unable to believe what they were hearing.

"Yes, Jimmy, but do you have any proof that is what

Martin is up to? I mean, we are humble Minnesotans. We don't want to get involved in any . . . ah rough stuff as it were."

"Mr. Sanderson, if these driving regulations are enforced, your company could stand to lose millions on the auto-glass that you provide."

Sanderson leaned back in his chair, pondering Jimmy's words and the hemorrhoid that was causing him much discomfort.

"And with even more to lose will be Mr. Steel. Accidents will decrease a thousand-fold, and ABC Towing will be wiped out."

"Waxhead, what do you plan to do about this Martin character!" Steel bellowed, as he leaned back in his chair also pondering the hemorrhoid that was causing him much grief.

"Gentlemen," Waxhead said, as he rose from his regal oaken chair with a bald eagle emblazed in gold on the back. He walked behind the chair and he began to stare off into the distance.

"You were about to say something?" Sanderson asked.

Waxhead shook himself from the image he had of himself at the lake sipping a cocktail and musing at the two bikini-clad women sunbathing themselves on the deck of his yacht.

"Ah, yes, I was." Again there was an awkward pregnant pause as Waxhead dreamed of the two bikini-clad women in his fantasy starting to rub coconut butter on his back.

"Waxhead, do you have a plan to deal with this Martin fellow?"

"Gentlemen, I do!"

Waxhead walked over to a large oaken cabinet that had images of what appeared to be northern Minnesota. He grabbed two large gold handles and opened the cabinet. Inside was a large flat-screen TV, given to Waxhead by Good Buy President Harry Wool. Harry Wool was cousins with Harry Steel and together their family had started the Steel Wool Company in Duluth. The younger Steel and Wool had gone on to bigger and badder things however.

Waxhead picked up what looked like a miniature wooden totem pole and clicked a button that was on top. It was a remote control that had been placed inside of a miniature totem pole, again appeasing Waxhead's longing for all things Midwestern, north woods and Indian.

"Gentlemen behold . . ."

As the men turned their attention to the television, an image of a couple water-skiing on a lake appeared. Immediately a narrator began to plug a time-share on Gull Lake.

"Yes, now you can have a time-share on some of Minnesota's most exclusive lake-front property. For only $10,000 a month, you can have . . . ."

"Waxhead!!! What are you doing? Trying to sell us a time-share?!!!" Sanderson screamed.

Waxhead sheepishly turned off the TV and sat back at his table.

"Ah, what I was trying to do was show you Gull Lake. This is where I will be luring Zeke Martin to this spring. What I plan to do is tell Zeke to come to my cabin as a reward for all the hard work he has been putting in.

Unfortunately for Zeke he will have a boating accident, and then . . . well, no more problems."

With that the men began to laugh a rather sinister laugh. Even James the butler enjoyed the idea.

"Oh, and by the way, it's really only $5,000 a month for the time-share. What do you guys think?"

Waxhead's proposal was greeted with sneering and immediate desertion by his guests. Waxhead thanked the men for their attention as they huffed their way out of the house. He then began to scheme about Zeke's demise . . . as well as how he could unload some great lake-front property on Gull Lake.

CHAPTER 9

As spring arrived Zeke was spending most of his time pulling old shacks out of the lakes as the ice began to thaw. It was another job that Waxhead had thrown his way to keep him busy, or as Zeke thought to keep him off track on his merging investigation.

Zeke again began to pour over the additional videotape he had received from the film department. He was quite surprised at what he was seeing; it was a video of the band Outta Control in concert at the Accel Arena. It showed Fred Dander in the mosh pit getting thrown around like a beach ball on the nose of seal. It was pathetic.

After moving through some of Fred Dander's home movies, and other independent film promos he was working on (Lord of the Ring Worm and Carrots of the Caribbean – the last film being a low-budget animated film involving carrots), Zeke finally came to the footage of traffic he wanted to document for the past few months.

Again the tapes showed more of the same merging chaos as the previous ones. This was overwhelming evidence and it was time to get it into the right hands – Mr. P's. Just as Zeke was about to finish the last videotape he saw something peculiar right at the end. He stopped and rewound the tape. On the far side of the Bloomington Ferry Bridge near the Old Shakopee Road exit he could see at the side of the road what appeared to be two red ABC tow trucks. Why would they be there? Clearly they were like vultures waiting for a crash to happen. More proof that something was definitely going on.

As Zeke began to look through another tape, the phone rang.

"Zeke Martin?"

"Yes."

"Senator Headache here – got a minute?"

Zeke hesitated, but then quickly thanked the congresswoman for calling.

"Zeke, I got your message about needing to put together some legislation regarding traffic laws and specifically merging. I think it's a great idea."

Zeke was accustomed to people these days paying him lip service. He knew however that with Headache on the transportation committee, he needed to interact with her as much as possible.

"Can you come down to my office so we can discuss it in further detail?" she asked.

Zeke agreed, and quickly slipped on a hat and coat which was unusual since he didn't own either article of clothing.

Before meeting with the senator, Zeke decided to pay a visit to one Willy Bradfordsson. Bradfordsson was a local manager for ABC Towing in an office building not too far from Zeke's house. Zeke would not pay a visit to Bradfordsson's office however; it was his house that Zeke was more interested in seeing.

Zeke could not believe his eyes as he pulled into Bradfordsson's driveway. Pulling into his driveway was not really a fair description of how long it was – more like searching for a rest stop before he actually reached the house was the feeling one had after driving for so long. The house was spectacular and it appeared to be completely made out of brick. It had limestone in the front entryway with ivy adoring the sides. It had the look of an elegant French chateau. As long as it took to drive up the driveway, it was even longer to walk up to the entryway. The sidewalk was bordered by hedges that had been meticulously shaped into various animals. Zeke was amazed at the detail of the bear, the giraffe, the lion, the elephant, but even more with the realistic features of the ameba.

Zeke pushed the doorbell and could hear what sounded like a Chinese gong being struck inside the house. Answering the door was a butler in full butler gear.

"May I help you, sir?"

"Yes, please. Willy Bradfordsson?"

"Ah yes, sir. May I inform him of who is calling?"

"Zeke Martin."

"Very good, sir. Please wait here in the foyer."

Zeke was stunned. The house was not only huge in size but the opulence, the incredible archway and all of the priceless pieces of art, sculpture and furniture were breathtaking. As equally as breathtaking was Willy Bradfordsson. Willy looked like a gas-station attendant who had been working all day on a car. He was covered in grease and stood in stark contrast to the beautiful house that surrounded him.

"Willy Bradfordsson?"

"Zeke Martin! Great to meet you. I've heard a lot about you."

"Boy, great place you got here, Willy."

"Ah it's nothing."

Willy motioned for Zeke to move over to the living room. Zeke peered around the entire room as if he were having some sort of spiritual vision from above.

"Like my paintin's?"

"Oh, yes they are incredible."

"Had that one flown in today straight from Vienna, Austria! What's the name of that one again, Saunders?" Bradfordsson asked, while snapping his fingers, hoping the frantic motion would jog his memory.

"That would be 'The Starry Night' by Vincent Van Gogh, sir."

"Van Gogh?!!! I thought it was Picasso!!! I don't want something from a third-rate artist!"

"Van Gogh is considered to be a genius and one of the leaders of the impressionistic period, sir."

"Leaders, huh. Give me a painting of some dogs playing poker and I'll show you some real art!" Bradfordsson laughed as he jabbed Zeke in the ribs with his elbow. Zeke's contempt for the uncouth character was rising by the minute.

"Anyway, whats can I do yaz for?"

"Well, Willy . . . Okay if I call you Willy?"

"My friends call me Willy, but you can call me Mr. Bradfordsson . . . Just kiddin'. Go ahead, Zeke."

"Well, I'm doing some research for the department regarding deer strikes, and I was wondering if I might impose upon you to get some numbers?"

"Oh, why sure, Zeke – anything to help the department. I'm sure Mr. Waxhead has you doing some really important things for the department, eh?"

Zeke noted a sarcastic tone in Willy's comment. Willy motioned for him to walk toward the back of the house. Willy pointed out various objects d'art and other mementos as they passed from the living room, through the dinning room and out onto a back balcony.

"Look at that, Zeke. Never would have happened without the good work of the men and women in the department."

Zeke beheld a breathtaking view of the enormous backyard. It had a driving range, an Olympic-sized swimming pool, and the largest brick barbecue he had ever seen. There were five or six teenage boys tearing around on various off-road vehicles.

"Hey, Jimmy, watch out for the . . ."

It was too late. Jimmy had plunged into the deep-end of the pool with his ATV. He quickly swam to the side and was pulled out by his friends.

"Like father like son, eh, Zeke?"

"Ah sure. Anyway, you seem to have a real reverence for the Department of Transportation?"

"Ah yah, they've been good to me and my family. If ever

I have a problem or question you can bet that Waxhead and his team will help me out."

Zeke continued his conversation with Willy, noting his almost undying allegiance to MNDOT. How Willy could afford the lifestyle he had was a mystery to Zeke, but he was going to do everything he could to find out. With that he bid Willy and his beautiful estate farewell.

Zeke quickly headed over to the capitol for his meeting with Senator Headache who was in town for a few days. While trying to put together a legal case to fight Waxhead, Zeke also thought that by going to his superiors, those in politics, he could perhaps make some changes that way. He did not know Headache, but knew she was a liberal and that usually meant they would be on your side for any kind of fight involving matters of pubic safety.

Phyllis Headache was a mystery to most people. She graduated first in her class from Harvard Law School, and immediately went into practice after passing the Bar exam. She was with a law firm in Boston for less than a year before she returned to her native Minnesota. It was presumed that she returned to Minnesota because of a scandal involving the most senior partner at the firm. The rumor was that she would do "favors" for Amory Flaghorn. Although Headache tried to convince everyone they were sexual favors, it turned out they were merely things like taking his dry-cleaning in or picking up his kids from school.

With the lack of anything to blackmail the senior partner with, so she could quickly rise to the top, she turned her attention on the good people of her home state. Once she returned to Minnesota she married Quinton Stalemate, or

Laughing Wolf, a leader of a local Ejimbway tribe in Savage. Stalemate was the CEO of Mystic Cake Casino where he made millions of dollars. Their marriage only lasted months, as Stalemate decided to move to Hollywood to further his career as an actor.

After the heartache of Stalemate, Headache decided to enter politics. She became the mayor of Savage for one year and then made a bid for state comptroller, but was easily defeated by the more experienced Victoria Allweed. Two years later she made a successful run after it was announced that Allweed was retiring to Bermuda to start a salmon farm. Bewildered voters had little choice but to put Headache-Stalemate into office.

Headache, who quickly dropped the Stalemate from her name, began a reign of fiscal governance that made her popular with the DFL (Democratic Fishing Liberals Party).

Two years later she was elected as a Congresswoman from the great state of Minnesota – and the rest was history, or in this case geography. It ended up that she picked the only congressional district that had no representation or anyone interested in running for a seat. Anyway, she was elected to congress and quickly used her legal savvy and her ex-husband's money to build a political machine the world would soon have to reckon with.

And so it was with this image in mind that Zeke stepped sheepishly into Congresswoman Headache's office.

"May I help you, sir?" the receptionist asked.

"Yes, I have an appointment with Congresswoman Headache."

"Yes, sir, and will you be using your membership card

today?"

"I'm sorry?" Zeke said, completely baffled.

"Or how did you choose to pay for your visit – cash, check? Did you happen to see our ad in the paper yesterday – five visits for only $1000?"

"Ah no, I didn't know I had to pay for it."

"Well you may want to become a member then. With membership you can have five visits for an annual fee of $350. With the membership you get preferred parking, a newsletter from Congresswoman Headache, a personal autographed picture each Christmas – or Hanukah, depending on your persuasion of course. You also get one hundred free tokens to use at Upchuck Cheeze Pizza – the kids really love that one."

"Ah, I was under the impression that meeting our representatives was free?"

"Yes, well . . ."

Just as the receptionist was going to speak, Congresswoman Headache rushed in from her office and greeted Zeke.

"Ah, Sally, don't worry about it. Ah, please . . . Zeke, correct?"

Zeke nodded to the affirmative.

"Zeke, please step into my office."

Zeke was amazed by the Congresswoman's office. It was adorned with pictures of her with various movers and shakers within the political world – there was even one of her with the mascot from Upchuck Cheeze Pizza. The one that caught his eye the most was one of her shaking hands with Harry Steel, the owner of ABC Towing.

"So, Zeke, what can I do you for?" Headache said, as she offered him a chair. She herself practically fell into her chair which resembled a giant wicker basket that he could imagine some king from Borneo sitting in.

"Like my chair? I got it from King Malaycan from Borneo. We did a little fact-finding trip over there last year. Wanted to see if there might be any business synergies between Minnesota and Borneo."

About the only synergies that existed were the ones created by Headache and the staff at a large beach resort near Kota Kinabalu.

"Well, Congresswoman, I have been building a case to send to the feds that will expose some problems we have here in Minnesota with traffic flow. We specifically have issues with regard to how we instruct and train drivers on merging."

"I see, Zeke. Do you mind if I call you Zeke?"

"Ah sure, that would be fine . . ."

"I love that name ZEKE! I had an uncle from New Germany that was named Zeke. He was Ezekiel Grumschuber. He was my mother's brother. My grandfather came over from Hanover in the late nineteenth century and were known as the Grumschubers. Thank the Lord that my Father changed their name to Headache, otherwise I would have had a real headache – if you know what I mean. I'm sorry about that, Zeke. Continue please."

"Well, I've been putting together a report as well as some videotape of high incident areas that confirm what I suspected about accidents here in Minnesota."

"I see, and accidents here seem a little high?"

"Well, yes. They are four hundred percent higher compared to the next highest ranked state."

"Hmmm, that is a little high."

"A LITTLE – It's absurd!"

"Yes, yes, I know what you mean. Care for any liquor . . . I mean beverage?"

"No, I'm fine, Congresswoman."

"Do you mind if I have something?"

"Ah, feel free."

Congresswoman Headache produced a crystal decanter that was in a lower cabinet drawer that looked like it could house gallons of whatever it contained. As she heaved it onto her desk, a mist of vodka seemed to spray Zeke like an early morning dew in Seattle.

After he recovered from almost choking on the Vodka spray, and the Congresswoman poured herself a coffee mug full of Vodka, he continued.

"Congresswoman, I would like you to read my . . ."

"Say no more, Zeke. I would like you to make a study of this problem immediately. I would like you to use everything at your resource and report back to me in no sooner than six months . . ."

"Congresswoman . . ."

"Let's make that a year. I want to get to the bottom of this problem . . . even if it takes several years. I want to find out what on earth could be causing this . . ."

"Ah, congresswoman, like I said I've already made a thorough investigation of the problem."

As Vodka began to dribble down the Congresswoman's chin, her eyes enlarged when she learned of Zeke's work. He plopped the telephone book sized report on her desk and her eyes became even more enlarged.

"I see. Okay. Let me review and get back to you then, Zeke. I appreciate the work you have done and I will get to this report right away. Say, it was great meeting you, Zeke. Can you please show yourself out?"

With that the Congresswoman grimaced as she picked up the report and walked through an adjoining door and quickly vanished. Zeke was a little perplexed and realized he was not going to get any more attention from the Congresswoman.

While in the capital building he quickly walked over to the business department to look up some records. He quickly confirmed his suspicions. Looking through the Secretary of State historical manuals for corporations on file, Zeke found the records for ABC Towing. From 1987 to 1994 the registered owner of ABC Towing was Quinton Stalemate.

Known for its immigrants from Sweden, Norway and Denmark, Minnesota now had another thing in common with the State of Denmark – something rotten.

That Friday evening, Zeke flew home to pick-up Gloria who was waiting by the curb with several packed bags and his fishing gear. Zeke quickly piled the cargo into the back of his extended cab and they were off in a blur.

He was well aware of the Friday night phenomenon in Minnesota where once the clock hit five, anyone who owned a cabin up north was on the road. He had calculated that the traffic during the summer months more than quadrupled on a Friday night, creating a traffic jam from the Twin Cities all the way to Duluth and other points north. The north woods were a welcome escape to Zeke who had grown up in Alabama and had enjoyed camping and fishing near Birmingham.

As Zeke and Gloria raced up 35E they immediately hit traffic just north of the cities. Zeke weaved in and out of traffic and eventually began to merge into the center lane. As he began to move he could see a woman in the far left lane also trying to enter the center lane. Both caught each other's eye and in a moment frozen in time, both instantly realized what the other one wanted. The moment when two drivers identify a piece of territory they both want to claim is when the world becomes an exhilarating place.

The woman in the other car was of English-Irish extract – she was organized and by Minnesota standards a good driver. She had a busy day and was heading out of town to meet her husband at their cabin near Gull Lake. When she saw the open lane her nostrils flared and she began to accelerate – it was at that moment that she made eye contact with Zeke in the far right lane.

Who would get to the center lane first?

Both drivers immediately hit the gas pedal. Zeke made a hard left turn and before the woman in the far left lane could react, he had made it to the center lane. The woman abruptly veered back to her "home" lane, shaken that she was not able to beat Zeke to the punch. The native Minnesotan's slow reaction had left her stunned and unable to merge as she had intended – her confidence was shattered. Zeke had escaped unscathed – if it weren't deer he was dodging, it was his fellow Minnesotan.

Zeke was pleased with his quick reaction and began to settle in for a long three hour drive up to Waxhead's cabin. Gloria, oblivious to what had happened, was reading Kierkegaard. It was like Mario Andretti chauffeuring Gertrude Stein during the Indianapolis 500. Apart from a quick rest stop, the pair arrived in less than three hours. As they pulled up the driveway to the "cabin," which was really a mansion by Zeke's standards, their mouths both dropped. They could not believe what they were seeing.

Waxhead's cabin, although having the north woods, pine log exterior, was the fanciest "cabin" they had ever seen. The driveway winded its way through beautiful woods that ended in a type of cul-de-sac overlooking the lake – this appeared to be the only home for miles around. The massive three story house had a fabulous view that seemed to stretch for miles.

Zeke slowly pulled out the bags from the truck while Gloria quickly unlocked the front door with the key that Waxhead had supplied them. Gloria was awestruck when she pushed open the door. While the walls were a beautiful white pine, the front entryway dropped down to an incredible living room that was surrounded by large windows that extended from the floor to the ceiling. What's more, part of the living room floor was actually made of glass so you could look down and see the water. This gave the sensation of being suspended over the lake.

They could then walk out onto a glass balcony that again played with their equilibrium. Until they got used to it, every time they walked to the balcony they had the feeling they would plunge gently into the cleansing waters of the lake.

After unpacking, the two had a quiet dinner and retired to the bedroom that was high atop a tower that looked even farther out onto the lake. As Zeke finished putting on his pajamas and brushing his teeth he began hunting for the bed.

"I assume there's a bed here somewhere?" he queried Gloria.

"Hmm, not sure," she replied, while she brushed her hair.

Zeke became enraptured of Gloria. There she was in a silhouette, brushing her brownish hair which had a golden gleam as she stared out the window. The window was a tall rectangular style that harkened back to the days of medieval castles. Zeke had to catch his breath – he was transported twenty years earlier to a time when he was so infatuated with Gloria, much the way many a young couple were when they were first married.

Gloria caught a glimpse of him looking at her in a nearby mirror. "Something the matter, Zeke?"

"Ah no, you just look . . . look beautiful."

Gloria didn't respond. She knew her silence would kill him. She knew he was dying to know what was on her mind right then. "Why don't you find some music to put on?" she said coyly, as she turned back to brush her hair.

"Great idea, but I think I'd like to find the bed first."

Zeke began to pace around the bedroom trying to figure out where the bed could be. He looked high and low – and no bed. "It must be in the wall, do you think?'

Gloria didn't reply, leaving the bed hunt up to Zeke. He

began to press his hands up and down the wall. The walls were of the same white pine boards that made up the rest of the house. Some of the walls had beautiful paintings that were signature of the area – conjuring up images of fowl hunts and sleepy fishing villages. As he felt along the wall for any sign of a switch or button he finally found what appeared to be a small box near one of the corners of the bedroom. It was a small pine box which blended into the wall. As Zeke fiddled with it he could see that it opened – and once opened it revealed a button. With rapt attention he pushed the button hoping he had found the bed. To his swift surprise he found himself on his back and on the bed that had shot out from the wall. The bed frame was in the style of the pine walls and not detectable, but once it was activated it immediately pushed out from the wall – unfortunately for Zeke he was right in the way of the errant projectile.

"Geez, Zeke, couldn't you create a mood first before you hop into bed. How 'bout some music?"

Zeke was still stunned from his encounter with the bed. "Ah, yah . . . sure, let me find something."

"Something romantic?"

As Gloria described the music she was looking for, Zeke managed to find the entertainment center and a large stack of CDs that were lined up high in a closet next to the main bedroom window. As he peered out the window he hoped none of the passing boaters had telescopic cameras or could somehow peer up into the bedroom. Despite the fact that the nearest water fairing craft was about ten miles away he decided to draw the curtains.

"How 'bout Led Zeppelin?"

Gloria frowned a comical frown and shook her head.

"How about some Sinatra or Tony Bennett?" she countered.

"I've got AC/DC, the Who . . . 'Won't Get Fooled Again' might get us in the mood."

As Zeke giggled to himself over his selection, he found an interesting CD. It was from superstar Brittany Spikes. It looked like it had been signed by her . . .

Dear Harry, glad you could join us backstage. Love Brittany.

"Hmm, that Waxhead really gets around." Zeke mumbled to himself. "Ah, here we go – how about Simply Red?"

Gloria agreed, and Zeke put on their greatest hits. Gloria sashayed over to the bed in a very skimpy nightgown. Zeke stared down at his pajamas, noting how conservative they were – but hey, he *was* conservative. He sauntered over to Gloria who was now lying on the bed in a very seductive way.

"Come over here, big boy."

Forgetting how to saunter, Zeke tripped over the bear rug that was near the bed, sending him chest-first into the nightstand next to the bed. When he sprung to his feet he had practically destroyed the pine stand. As he brushed himself off he noticed a picture that had been placed in the drawer of the nightstand, but was now visible in the rubble he had created.

"Hmm, what's that on the floor?" Gloria asked.

"It's a picture of something or other"

As Zeke examined it more closely he became a little ill. It

was a picture of Walter Zimroid, the president of DEF Towing shaking hands with Waxhead. Another example of Waxhead's under-the-table partnerships.

The next morning after breakfast, Zeke and Gloria decided to take the little motor boat that Waxhead had left for their use that weekend. As he helped Gloria into the boat and untied the line holding it to the pier, he could see on the other side of the sprawling property what appeared to be a boathouse attached to the side of the main house. He wondered what kind of craft could be housed there. He shook his head and started up the motor.

The morning water on the lake was calm and glassy, with the sun just poking its head above the beautiful blue pines that lined the shore. He and Gloria were in a good mood – the evening before had set the tone and life seemed new again. As Zeke cruised along he could feel the cool breeze through his hair. Gloria smiled at him, ignoring the fact that he had placed an open jar of worms on her side of the boat. The wind created by the boat was causing the worms to fly out at a tremendous rate. Gloria had learned over the years to not focus on these eccentricities of Zeke. She preferred to look at him for all his good qualities – his kindness, his handiness, being a good provider, and the only one she knew who could figure out how to program the timer on her electric hair curler.

Like Zeke, Gloria had also been the eye of affection from a potential suitor as of late. Sensing that Zeke had lost interest in her, she subconsciously or semi-consciously had become flirty and had found herself in provocative conversations with her local chief librarian at the Burnsville library. Mr. McNulty had the intellectual acumen that Zeke sometimes lacked – not that Zeke was dumb, it was just that he didn't share her passion for literature and culture. With Bob McNulty she could talk to him about almost anything. Like Zeke however, she could not bring herself to cheat on her spouse – the commitment had been too long and there was no point putting herself in a compromising position – and beside, Zeke had started to show more interest in her as of late.

As Zeke killed the motor, they glided slowly into a little secluded inlet. After coming to a sudden stop, courtesy of a large rock Zeke had failed to notice, Gloria pulled out a Thermos and poured Zeke a cup of coffee. The scene was tranquil and both began to relax as they cast their reels. As Zeke took a sip of his Sumatran, the blaring horn of a huge yacht caused him to spill half of it into his lap. Zeke began to scream as the scolding hot coffee ran down his pant leg. Gloria rose from her seat to help him and they both began to tip the boat, sending each other careening overboard. As they came to the surface they were greeted by the yacht and its owner – Harry Waxhead!

"Zeke . . . Gloria! What are you guys doing in the water down there?"

"We thought this would be a better way of catching fish."

"That's ridiculous! Here, climb up the rope ladder."

Zeke helped Gloria climb up the ladder and quickly followed behind her.

"Mr. Waxhead, what are you doing here?"

"Oh, I thought I'd meet you guys – do a little

entertaining."

"You're staying at the cabin?"

"No, the cabin's a little cramped for us. We're staying over there."

Waxhead was pointing to a mansion on the other side of the lake that dwarfed the huge complex they were currently staying at.

"C'mon, let's have a little fun, Zeke!"

With that, Waxhead escorted Zeke and Gloria on a tour of his yacht. It was a state of the art luxury yacht/cruiser that could reach forty miles per hour. He showed them to his stateroom which, like his mansion in St. Paul, was outfitted with all things Wisconsin. Mrs. Waxhead was in the room doing her nails.

"Oh, hello, you two. I'm so glad you could drop by," she said, with tight clenched lips looking like a demented clown with lipstick that seemed to be gooped on beyond the border of her lips. Gloria did not suffer fools and never got along with Mrs. Waxhead.

"Great to see you too, Zelda. Read any good books lately?"

"C'mon, my dear, you know with my busy social calendar and keeping up the house I have no time for such idle indulgences."

Gloria smiled and nodded her head in mock agreement.

"I'm surprised you have any time to read these days, given your condition," Mrs. Waxhead said.

"My condition? What condition is that?"

"I'm not sure, but you look so tired and worn out, dear."

Gloria stood up tall. "I feel perfectly fine."

"I guess it must be all those hours your husband is working. Perhaps you're not sleeping well with him out at all hours of the night?"

"No, I sleep rather well. Zeke does too."

"Sorry, dear, it must be something else causing those wrinkles then."

After the tour, Waxhead showed Zeke and Gloria some water skiing equipment, and offered them an afternoon of fun on skis. They had done a little waterskiing over the years but nothing like this. They jumped at the idea. Gloria especially had something to prove to Mrs. Waxhead.

After getting into the water and putting on their skis, Zeke gave Waxhead the signal to apply the throttle. With a sudden surge the pair began to feel themselves lifted from the water. It was like riding a bicycle and they quickly got their balance as they began to pick up speed. The two looked at each other with big gleaming smiles like little kids who were sharing a secret. They enjoyed the sudden rush as they gained full speed, bouncing back and forth and basking in the cool spray that was being generated. This was freedom, and for the first time in a long time Zeke felt free – free of almost every care. Well, maybe that was what Waxhead wanted.

As they buzzed by a pier they could see Waxhead waving his hand in a circular motion like he wanted to go by the pier again. Zeke responded with the a-okay and Waxhead continued to turn the boat around. As they came by for their second pass of the pier they could sense that Waxhead had put the boat in full throttle and they were beginning to bounce almost uncontrollably. Zeke tried to wave to

Waxhead, but the director kept his focus on the horizon. As they began to swing around they could see that Waxhead was purposely trying to catapult them into the pier – both Zeke and Gloria began to scream out to Waxhead but to no avail. They could see Mrs. Waxhead coolly waving back to them, smiling and nodding her head in apparent delight.

Zeke and Gloria began to panic. They were being slingshot toward the pier and almost simultaneously their lines snapped. They were now hurtling their way toward the pier with little hope of being able to stop. Zeke looked over at Gloria and immediately pushed her over so she would fall into the water. He knew that would hurt her but it would be better than barreling into the oncoming woodwork. Luckily for Gloria she bounced once and landed into the water with no further discomfort.

As Zeke neared the pier he could see a fast approaching motorboat that was running parallel with the pier and heading out to the lake. He quickly took his snapped line, formed a lasso and swung it out over the back of the motorboat. The line snagged the anchor that was in back and held firm.

As the motorboat headed into the lake it took Zeke with it, and he quickly swung around just missing the pier by inches. As Zeke pulled hard on the line it accidentally pulled the anchor off the boat and it quickly sank to the bottom. The boat became strained from the weight of the anchor and the engine began to smoke as the boat tried to force itself along the water.

The boat's driver, a short, bespectacled gentleman turned in dismay to find his motor practically in flames. He immediately turned for shore with Zeke in tow. Zeke tried to yell to the man but the terrible grinding sound of the engine made it impossible to be heard.

The panicked driver of the boat frantically steered toward a nearby beach and immediately beached himself there and quickly jumped overboard. Zeke, in hot pursuit came tumbling onto the beach in a pile of tangled line and other sundry items that had washed up onto the shoreline.

The Waxheads immediately pulled near the beach.

"Why, Martin, that was positively spectacular, my boy. You are resourceful indeed!"

Zeke looked at Waxhead with as much anger as he could muster. Clearly Waxhead was trying to kill him, and he didn't even seem to care how obvious he was. Zeke shouted to Waxhead to quickly retrieve Gloria and they were soon reunited together in the stateroom of the yacht. Mr. and Mrs. Waxhead quickly tried to make amends.

"I'm terribly sorry about that, ol' boy. That must have been a terrible fright for the pair of you."

Zeke was silent, preferring to look around for something heavy to heave at the man.

"Look here, we'll definitely have to make it up to you. Join us up on deck as soon as you change back into your clothes."

Both Waxhead and a giggling Mrs. Waxhead made their exits.

"Gloria, look at this line I kept. I think it was tampered with. It looks frayed."

Gloria nodded with disbelief. "But why? Why would Waxhead do something like this?"

"I have a feeling I know why. C'mon, let's go upstairs."

The two made their way up on deck and were startled at what they saw. It was a complete buffet with all types of seafood and pasta, and various other types of delicacies. Clearly Waxhead meant to impress.

"Get me those deer reports ready, Zeke, and you'll find more fantastic times like this. Here, have some champagne."

Waxhead motioned to his butler to pour both Zeke and Gloria some champagne. Zeke feigned a smile only to try and gain Waxhead's confidence. He didn't want to let on that he suspected Waxhead was trying to do away with him.

"Hey, Zeke, I hope there are no hard feelings? By the way, here's my key ring to the boathouse at the cabin. This one opens the boathouse and this one is for the ignition for the boat that's in there. I think you will be duly impressed. Why don't you and Gloria give her a test drive tomorrow?"

Zeke nodded, appreciating the bribe he was being offered. Now it was time to stuff himself on lobster and shrimp.

The next morning Zeke and Gloria made up their minds to try the lake again – this time with Waxhead's prized speedboat. After a glorious breakfast of sausage and egg at Phil's in the main town of Gull Lake, they decided to putter around a bit in some of the shops. Gloria loved antiques and so they spotted a little shop that had an old seafaring look to it and decided to enter.

As they browsed around the shop they were introduced, almost against their will, to the shop's owner.

"T.J. McBride at your service. How can I help you folks

today?"

"Ah, we're just browsing," the semi-angered Zeke replied.

T.J. McBride's Antiques had been a mainstay amongst the citizens and visitors to Gull Lake for over forty years. The business itself was more than eighty years old; originally name E.J. McBride's Antiques after T.J.'s grandfather. T.J. took over the business when his ailing grandfather began to become a bit senile. Not a fan of the invention of the motorcar, E.J. took to throwing antiques at cars that would pass by. This not only put a dent in the business but killed the Gull Lake mayor, Bill Stevens in 1959. As Stevens was passing by in his brand new Mercedes Benz, his windshield was struck by an eighteenth century Prussian vase which caused him to spin and then drive into Gull Lake itself. It was at that point that grandson T.J. decided to take over the business. Not surprisingly the business made money the following year.

"Hey, Zeke, look at this adorable spice rack. It's painted with all these wonderful images of a farmhouse with all of the different spices labeled."

"Yes, my dear lady, and it's only thirty-five dollars. It was made in 1902 and was built on a farm near here – it's really priceless though."

Zeke rolled his eyes and wished he had never set foot in the establishment. As he did his best to avoid the owner, he noticed an interesting photograph on the wall – it was Waxhead with his arm around T.J.

"Hey, ah, Mr. McBride, can you tell me about this picture over here?"

T.J., practically stumbling over himself was hoping Zeke was referring to one of the antique pictures on the wall that were not selling well as of late.

"Oh, ah, that's just me and Mr. Waxhead."

"You friends with Waxhead?"

"Ah, yah sure, you could say that. He's a kind of a patron here – he's made quite a few purchases. He's a real good guy."

Zeke nodded his head, not believing that T.J. was really a friend of Waxhead's. "I think we'd better go, Gloria. We've only a few hours on the lake today."

Zeke motioned for Gloria to walk to the door. She, noting Zeke's odd expression, decided she probably should do as he was requesting. As they walked out the door, Gloria paused.

"Oh, Zeke – I left my purse in there."

"I'll get it."

As Zeke walked back into the shop he noticed that T.J. wasn't around. He looked for Gloria's purse toward the back of the shop where the spice rack was. As he spotted the purse he could hear someone in the backroom. They were mumbling something and Zeke figure they were probably on the phone.

"Yah, they were just here – Martin and his wife."

Zeke could hear the voice of T.J. McBride talking on the phone. "Yah, anyway, I thought I'd let you know."

As Zeke heard McBride hang-up, he decided to grab Gloria's purse and quickly exit the shop. He met up with Gloria on the sidewalk and they began to walk back to the cabin. Walking through the town they noticed it was eerily quiet. They could also see window shades being lowered and doors closing as they walked by.

"It's interesting that as soon as I mentioned Waxhead's name to the shopkeeper back there, the whole town seems to have gone into a lockdown. What's going on here?"

"Maybe we should just head home, Zeke?"

"No, I need to find out what's going on. Let's spend a few hours on the lake. Maybe we'll find something out."

Gloria, not exactly happy with Zeke's plan, nodded her head in mock agreement.

"Do you think Waxhead is tied in with the Mafia?" Gloria asked, fearing the worst.

"It's hard to say. One thing that's clear is that he's on the take."

After arriving back at the cabin, Zeke and Gloria got into their swim suits and prepared for an afternoon on the lake. Gloria packed some sandwiches while Zeke went to prepare the boat. As Zeke walked down into the basement, he found a door which he thought would lead to the boathouse. As he turned the knob and pushed the door through, he was startled to find a room full of boxes. And these were not ordinary boxes; they were boxes full of cash. There must have been millions of dollars in the room. Zeke looked through a few of the boxes but decided he better not stay. He was confused as to why the money was there. Surely Waxhead would know that either he or Gloria might stumble onto the money? Zeke decided not to inform Gloria of the discovery. He knew that would really send her into a panic – or a coma. One of the two.

Zeke closed the door and walked to the next one. As he

opened it he could see the shining reflection of water on the walls – it must be a hallway to the boathouse, he thought to himself. Still shaken by the money in the other room, he slowly made his way into the boathouse. As he came into the boathouse he was greeted by an awe-inspiring sight – it was a beautiful, silver chromed speedboat. It was thirty-three feet long and looked like it could fly.

Zeke had been acquainted with speedboats ever since his youth in Alabama, but he had never seen anything like this. This would be fun. He quickly pulled the tarp off the boat and jumped in. The boat was immaculate and well taken care of. This was one of his dreams, and Waxhead of all people was making it come true.

Zeke prepared the boat and directed Gloria via cell-phone on how to get down to the boathouse. She arrived shortly afterward with a nice picnic basket in hand. He helped her into the boat, quickly started up the "beast" as he referred to it, and applied some gas. Within a minute they were skimming along the waves of the lake – both with large grins on their faces.

After an hour of splashing themselves silly, leaving their clothes soaking wet they decided to lay anchor by a sandbar and have their lunch. As they came toward the sandbar they spotted another boat, and began to wave to the occupants. The couple in the other boat waved back but had rather odd expressions of agitation on their faces – as if Zeke and Gloria had intruded upon their private spot. The man quickly picked up a phone and began to speak into it with a rather angered look. He started up the boat, quickly floored the gas and sped away. Zeke and Gloria were used to this form of "Minnesota Nice" and initially ignored it. What was unusual though was they began to notice a complete lack of other boats on the lake.

"Where did everybody go?" Gloria pondered aloud.

Zeke shook his head as he threw over the anchor. Gloria offered him a ham on rye and they relaxed in the leather deck chairs that adorned the boat. Zeke grabbed a cola and quickly gobbled down his sandwich. The two began to fantasize about their adventure.

"I wonder if Scott and Zelda lived like this?" Gloria said with a dreamy look on her face.

"Scott and who?"

"Scott and Zelda from the Great Gatsby."

"The Great what?"

"The Great Gatsby! Surely you have read that immortal novel by F. Scott Fitzgerald?"

"Is he related to George C. Scott?"

"No, F. Scott Fitzgerald. How can you confuse the last name Fitzgerald with the last name Scott?"

"Well, they both have Scott in their name and an abbreviation."

"And the fact that the Scott and the abbreviation are in a different order didn't occur to you?"

"Nothing much occurs to me when I'm sitting on the most beautiful boat in the most beautiful, pristine lake with the most beautiful woman in the world."

Gloria appreciated Zeke's comment – noting what a convenient way it was to get out of the argument.

"Well, let's head back and beat that traffic."

"Do we have to go back so soon?" Gloria said coyly, as

she lay provocatively on the deck of the boat.

Zeke caught her drift and rose to his feet. The feigned Errol Flynn look on his face brought out a loud giggle in Gloria. He marched over to her with his puffed out chest and his fists clenched in order to make his biceps bulge at the proper moment.

"My goodness, Mr. Scott, you do look rather manly."

"Yes, my good lady, you look like you are in need of a good man. Well, I am here to provide my services."

As they both giggled they soon became quiet. Things had not been perfect for the past twenty years but they still loved each other. With this thought in mind, Zeke's expression turned serious. Gloria could see in his eyes that he really meant business. Her smile went from a giggling teenager to a mature receptive woman. Zeke moved slowly so as not to appear he was overstepping his bounds. Gloria blinked her eyes coyly as to give her man the green light.

He straightened up and smiled, never wanting Gloria to feel like this was an obligation. She smiled again to confirm that this was no obligation. His smile changed from one of happiness to appreciation. Gloria nodded in a thankful nod, knowing that his smile of appreciation was for no instant gratification, but for appreciation of what she meant to him.

He moved forward and bent down over Gloria. He offered his hand to which she placed hers delicately on top of his. He began to stroke her hair and said nothing. After twenty years there was nothing that needed to be said by either one of them.

For a brief instant there was a boat with a water-skier that passed by, which slightly distracted Zeke from the moment. As the boat swooshed by, he returned back to Gloria, completely unaware that it was Waxhead who had just swooshed by.

"I love . . ."

Gloria put her finger to Zeke's lips before he could finish. This was a magic moment and she did not want it ruined by mere human words. He understood, and with that began to seize the moment by rising above Gloria and signaling that he would like to "come aboard the Love Boat." Gloria saluted and Zeke did in kind, and began to mount the queen of his Love Boat. As he did so, he slipped on a puddle of water and sent them both careening overboard into the lake.

As the two surfaced they exploded with laughter. Any other couple might have been angered by their spouse's sloppiness or clumsiness, but the moment was too funny and was exactly what they both needed. Zeke quickly found the step ladder and hoisted Gloria into the boat with him. They both landed on the deck of the boat and again exploded with laughter. The moment was more magical than if they had made love. Their spirits had connected as if they were in college again. Love-making, as great as it would have been, took a backseat to the true fun they were having.

Sex was not everything, and although they both often thought that it was, it was being together that was most important. It was being a couple. It was at that point that Zeke realized that there would be no one else for him. No matter how beautiful a woman might be, it didn't replace the friendship and loyalty he had for Gloria.

He silently grabbed Gloria by the hand and lifted her up.

He gave her a long passionate kiss as he held her in his arms and then laid her in one of the deck chairs. He pulled back and looked into her eyes. There was nothing that needed to be said, no other action necessary. He smiled and stood up. He walked over to the front of the boat and turned the key in the ignition. The boat quickly hummed its faithful tune and they were soon speeding away from the sandbar.

As Zeke floored the gas with all the adrenaline of a Minnesota Norseman football player, he began to smell the faint odor of kerosene. As they zoomed along the waves of Gull Lake the smell became stronger and stronger. Gloria shrieked and Zeke turned in horror to find their motor was completely engulfed in flames. Gloria panicked and ran over to Zeke, not having ever encountered such an out of control fire before.

Zeke turned the boat toward the cabin and debated as to whether or not to try and make it to shore – or to just abandon the boat. The engine began to whine and sputter and Zeke decided he wouldn't take any further chances. He immediately grabbed Gloria by the hand and pulled her atop the side of the boat. He simultaneously screamed for her to jump as he pulled her into the water.

As Zeke and Gloria surfaced, for the fourth time that weekend, they could see the boat skimming along with an engine that sounded like a possessed banshee. It headed towards the town pier, and Zeke and Gloria gasped as they could see people standing near the edge trying to find out what the strange noise was. They screamed as loud as they could to alert the onlookers to stop on-looking. As soon as the people could make out the boat speeding toward them with a massive fire in the back, they panicked and ran from the pier. Just as several of them cleared off, the boat pierced the end of the pier and exploded into a large fireball.

All at once it seemed like everyone from a fifty mile radius was in the area inspecting the damage. Before Zeke and Gloria knew what had happened, a police boat was circling around them with one of its occupants barking something inaudible to them.

"All right, you two. Haven't you caused enough problems here this weekend?" a large surly man yelled into his bullhorn, only several feet away from the perturbed and bedraggled boat nicks.

"You can see that your bullhorn is almost in my face, can't you!!!" yelled back an equally angered Zeke.

"That'll be enough from you! Now grab a hold of this life raft and we'll pull you aboard."

Zeke and Gloria quickly complied and were hoisted onto the boat. Without so much as a word of "how are you?" or "can we get you anything?" Zeke and Gloria were whisked off toward town. Zeke studied the man that had helped them climb aboard. He was a burley gentleman with grey thinning hair, looking to be in his fifties. He had a potbelly and his appearance was that of someone who had little interaction with crime fighting. He bore captain's stripes and so Zeke assume that was his rank. He was not quite sure however why a police captain would have come upon the scene so quickly – unless he had already been cruising around or perhaps already summoned.

The man driving the boat appeared to be not much older than twenty. He sat silently behind the wheel as the captain screamed out orders which it seemed the junior officer was ignoring. The captainappeared to be barking orders of a nautical nature, but they were ones Zeke had not quite heard before, or at least in the context they were being spoken.

"All right, Sanders, pull it into the dock and secure the jibe. Drop the anchor and ensure the moorings are hoisted."

Again the driver appeared to pay him no attention. As the boat was docked, the police officers escorted Zeke and Gloria to a nearby squad car. Walking to the car, the pair was greeted with jeers from the nearby crowd that had gathered.

"Trying to ruin our quiet lake-side town, will yah? Go back to the city where you belong, you . . . you *city* person!!!" yelled a kindly old lady, who could barely hold on to the walker she used to support herself.

"Trying to blow up our pier, huh? Better luck next time, you cowardly, yellow-belly sapsucker!" came the odd curse from an elderly man sporting a tuxedo.

Zeke did a double-take, trying to understand why the crowd was so hostile, and why a man in a tuxedo was calling him a sapsucker.

"Alright, you two, into the car!"

As Zeke and Gloria were shoved into the backseat of the patrol car they began to feel they were in some sort of an avant-garde film. It was if they had landed into some kind of French film where they were the only sane ones and the entire village was crazy. This was no film, and this was not France, however, and Zeke and Gloria were at a loss as to what was happening.

"Hey, Sarge, can I put on the siren?"

"Sure, go ahead, Einstein."

Zeke and Gloria smiled at the sergeant's insult but found out later that the other officer's name was in fact Einstein. Zeke began to make small talk . . .

"Sarge, huh? I thought those were captain's stripes on your sleeve?"

"Well, they are . . . if you're a police officer in Albania."

The two officers began to giggle uncontrollably and Zeke decided to keep quiet. As the two men laughed they collided with a nearby car as they merged onto the main street of the town. When they neared the police station, the officer attempted to move into another lane and promptly hit another car, this time sending the vehicle and its occupants into a stop sign.

"Hmm, you better call ABC towing ASAP when we get to the station."

As they pulled into the parking lot of a small building, they could see from signage that it was the Gull Lake police department. The pair were quickly pulled from the backseat.

Zeke and Gloria were tugged and pulled through the station by the officers who had clearly never had the experience or training on how to handle and move a prisoner.

"Captain Potluck, they're here!" Sergeant Billdarp screamed. As he did so, almost immediately a man stepped out from behind a door and approached the pair. He was portly, and like Sergeant Billdarp was in his fifties.

"Ah, good work, men! It looks like we've more than paid for our salaries by bringing in these lawbreakers."

"How are we lawbreakers?!!!" Zeke screamed.

The sergeant immediately pulled and jerked Zeke by the arm, trying to restrain him from such a disrespectful comment.

"We've had our eye on you all weekend, Mr. Martin. First it was the water-skiing trick, and then it was the rude comments you made to the mayor's wife this morning and then now – blowing up boats – what's up with that?"

"What a minute, back up here – we didn't make any rude comments to anyone?"

"You don't remember when you pulled up to the sandbar this afternoon. The mayor called to inform us that you were making advances to his wife."

"You've got to be kidding!" Gloria nearly screamed. "Zeke did nothing of the sort. We saw some people on a boat and we waved to them."

"Wave to them, huh? Must have been a special wave, hey, Mr. Martin?"

"Okay, this is getting out of hand. I demand to see a lawyer this instant!"

"I don't think that will be necessary, Zeke."

Zeke and Gloria turned around and were astonished to find Waxhead in the front doorway.

"Chief Potluck, these are friends of mine. I apologize for some of the incidents that have occurred but I assure you they are okay."

Zeke and Gloria were amazed to see Waxhead, and to see what kind of reaction the rest of the police officers had toward him. It was dead silent, until Potluck broke the ice.

"Are you sure, Mr. Waxhead?"

Waxhead silently nodded, to which Potluck quietly

nodded back with a smile.

"Anything you say, Mr. Waxhead. We're happy to help you in any small way we can. Boys, release the Martins."

With that, Waxhead waved over what appeared to be his chauffer, who walked Zeke and Gloria to his limousine.

"Zeke, Gloria – I apologize. This has not been your weekend has it? I was hoping you would have a relaxing stay with us up here in the north woods – and look what's happened . . . What a pity."

Zeke had a sick feeling in his stomach as he listened to Waxhead's feigned words of sympathy. He was even sicker when he began to realize that the man that was water-skiing near them when the boat caught fire was Waxhead. It was hard to see from a distance, and the sun had put him in shadows, but he knew that silhouette. It must have been him. Waxhead wanted him dead, and if the day before was any indication this was certainly the icing on the cake.

"Zeke, I apologize again for what happened. Look, here's a couple of tickets to tomorrow night's Minnesota Triples game. They're playing the New York Hankeys."

Zeke hesitantly took the tickets but gave Waxhead a glare that could only mean one thing – he was onto Waxhead.

"Yah, those are for the suite."

"Suite?" Zeke queried.

"Ah, yah, ABC towing has a suite at the Megadome. We caught that wild game last week where the Triples came back from a seven run deficit to beat the Cleveland Palefaces 11-9. Great game, great game!"

Zeke and Gloria were silent for the rest of the trip back

to the cabin. When dropped off by Waxhead they quickly gathered their belongings, hopped into Zeke pick-up and headed out of Gull Lake like there was no tomorrow.

After fighting with Gloria over the quality of the Hamburger Helper of late, Zeke decided he would bring Malaysia to the Triples game. Besides, Malaysia was working on the case with him and it was important that she be there to help pick up any clues. After work that evening, Zeke drove Malaysia to the Megadome. They were greeted at the front gate and told to drive directly into the underground parking. A valet took Zeke's deer-beaten truck and showed them an elevator to take up toward the ballpark. After being instructed to hit "9" Zeke and Malaysia giggled at each other, noting the absurd amount of pomp and circumstance being thrown their way.

As they reached the ninth floor, the door opened and they were greeted by Minneapolis mayor Tom Plenty. Zeke liked Plenty and saw him as a good-natured, down-to-earth, multi-millionaire Minnesotan. Actually, Mayor Plenty had no clue who Zeke was, and just pointed to a stadium worker as he hopped onto the elevator.

"Good evening, sir. Harold's the name, and I will be happy to escort you good people to your luxury box," said the kindly old stadium worker.

"Thanks, Harold." Zeke smiled as he looked over at an equally impressed Malaysia.

"Like I said last time, you sure know how to show a girl a good time, Zeke Martin!'

Zeke blushed and laughed. He began to think that

brining Malaysia to the game was not a good idea. He could tell his feelings were too strong for her, and things might get extremely complicated if he didn't watch out.

Harold quickly showed Zeke and Malaysia to the Waxhead's opulent box. As the two stepped into the room they were amazed at what they saw. It was a luxury box for sure – well-stocked bar and refrigerator, beautiful leather furniture with various renowned works of art. The room had large flat screen televisions for those who wanted to see the action up close or for those who cared little for the action on the field and wanted to see alternate programming. There was even a hot-tub and a sauna – it was everything Zeke had dreamt about. This was somewhere a man could go and die happy.

Right behind football, baseball was Zeke's favorite sport. He did like Rubleule, an ancient Moroccan form of rugby mixed with polo and camels, but baseball had always been a close contender for the number two spot. As a boy he enjoyed going to the park where his dad would throw baseballs at him. He did eventually get a bat, which helped, and he soon began to learn the game well. He never forgot the home-run he hit in Little-League that went through Mr. Gardner's kitchen window, knocking a frying pan with grease over and setting the whole house ablaze. They were good times and he loved the sport.

As Zeke and Malaysia settled in to watch the game, Harry Waxhead came into the room.

"Hi, Zeke, hi, Malaysia! Glad you two could catch the game tonight."

Zeke nodded, while Malaysia offered a bright smile and

a wave. Waxhead walked over to the bar and poured himself a shot of whiskey.

"Say, I just wanted to ask you, Zeke, about that report you are working on . . . the one about merging."

Zeke again nodded in silence, wondering what Waxhead wanted.

"If I could take a look at that it would be terrific. I'd like to see if I could help you out there. By the way, where do you keep it?"

"Oh, in a safe place."

"Say, why don't I have Jimmy swing by and pick it up."

"Nope, we're good."

Zeke's reluctance to divulge any information was driving Waxhead crazy. Waxhead paced around the room for a while like a caged animal about to strike, but Zeke and Malaysia paid no attention to him, keeping their focus on the Triple's play on the field. Finally, not having any luck with obtaining the information he was after, Waxhead walked out of the luxury box in a huff. Zeke and Malaysia giggled, truly enjoying the tizzy they had put the director in.

As the game continued, Zeke received a call from Fred Smithsonian from the Prahnpratvinchalnuralpravin, Smithsonian, Wilson and Partners law firm. He informed Zeke that the report and the information he had supplied them with, gave them enough evidence of a conspiracy and would be prosecuting Director Waxhead for fraud and failing to protect the public safety.

Zeke was thrilled to hear the news, and made arrangements to meet Smithsonian the next day to go over the case.

CHAPTER 10

Zeke arrived at the law firm of Prahnpratvinchalnural-pravin, Smithsonian, Wilson and Partners and was surprised by the humble appearance of the office. It was right next door to the county race track, and to say it was Spartan was an understatement. As Zeke parked in the rear of the building he was greeted by a pack of wild dogs that sniffed and pulled him from one side to the other. He tripped and found himself sprawling on the ground. He quickly picked himself up, grabbed a nearby bone and flung it out into an adjacent field. The dogs immediately pounced on the bone's new location as if being pulled by a giant magnet.

Zeke brushed himself off and surveyed the area. There were two beaten-up chicken coops, a wooden trough of water that looked pretty murky, and what appeared to be a small barn. Taking a quick glance within the barn revealed a cow and a few goats and nothing much else, except one fence dividing the goats from the cow.

As Zeke walked back toward the office he noticed for the

first time that on the other side of the law office was a restaurant. He initially thought it was a part of the office building when he first drove in, but could see now that it was a separate building. Upon closer inspection he could see it was a Thai restaurant – "The Prahnprat-vinchalnuralpravin Palace."

"Ah, Zeke, I could see you wandering around back here so decided to come and get you." Fred Smithsonian waved to Zeke from a side door to the law office.

Zeke, still puzzled by the whole complex, walked slowly over to Smithsonian.

"Yah, that's Mr. P's restaurant. Not only is he a top-notch lawyer, but a very adept businessman as well. His family runs the restaurant."

Zeke nodded and smiled, admiring the entrepreneurial spirit of Mr. P.

Smithsonian showed him into a dining area that was arrayed with what appeared to be a Thai buffet. The room was adorned with bright red drapery covering the walls. There were several golden statues of the Buddha. The warm and exotic smell of incense immediately greeted his nose as he walked toward the dining area.

"Zeke, feel free to help yourself to the buffet. It's compliments of Mr. P. It's from his restaurant next door."

Zeke, feeling hungry, immediately grabbed a plate and started helping himself to the Asian delicacies. As he assembled something resembling a miniature scale of the Matterhorn, Mr. P walked into the room with Fred Smithsonian. As the two men watched Zeke ladle on the food, Smithsonian encouraged Zeke to pace himself and to have a seat. Mr. P laughed at Zeke's gusto for Thai cuisine, and motioned for him to take it a bit slower.

On a large dark cherry wood table where Mr. P motioned for Zeke to sit, were piles of neatly organized papers. Zeke assumed they were papers they were using to prepare for court proceedings.

"Wow, looks like you have been working hard on our case," Zeke said, with a bright smile.

"Actually no, most of these are Mr. P's manuscript for his next book that we have been working on."

Smithsonian went on to explain that Mr. P was writing an autobiography about his life as an immigrant from Thailand. The book would detail his life as a young man, struggling to leave the dangerous golden triangle in northern Thailand, hiking through treacherous jungles and mountains to get to Bangkok.

Mr. P's life in Bangkok was a series of obstacles that saw him maneuver through life as a drug kingpin, a pimp, a tuk-tuk driver, a temple security guard and a durian picker. It was while he was picking durians that he decided to study Thai law. So during the night in the durian fields, he would study by candlelight. With the income he had from durian picking he went onto law school where he was first in his class. He rose to the top of his field in the Chalpriah, Saranathan and Smith law firm, representing clients like Royal Thai Durian, Royal Imperial Tuk Tuk Service and Thai Airways.

Mr. P's past caught up with him when a local drug lord in Chaing Mai began harassing his family after he found out that Mr. P had become a successful lawyer in Bangkok.

When Mr. P got word of his family's plight, he immediately had them moved down to Bangkok with him. After finding out about the escape, the angered drug lord put a contract out on Mr. P and so he fled Thailand and sought refuge in the United States.

It was an amazing story and one Zeke was very interested in, but what had more of his attention was the case against the state of Minnesota. Smithsonian began to fumble around with many of the papers that had been scattered around the table. Zeke's confidence in Smithsonian was already low, and seeing how disorganized he was did not help matters.

"Okay, let's see here. Now the main thrust of our case is that we feel certain members of the department have concealed from the public the section of the traffic laws that pertain to merging?"

Zeke nodded as he watched the frenzied Mr. Smithsonian shuffle papers with one hand and write notes with the other. A continually smiling Mr. P looked on.

"Now, we aim to prove that their motivation for such a grievous act is that they conspired to use the lack of regulation to create an atmosphere of unsafe driving creating an unusually high number of accidents, resulting in high towing revenues – and the revenue created from the towing created substantial kick-backs to certain government officials."

Smithsonian made this statement, while simultaneously scooping a spoonful of Thai chicken salad with his right hand, writing a note in Thai for Mr. P with his left – and at the same time reading the prepared document. Zeke began to feel a little sick in his stomach and wondered if it were the Thai cuisine or watching Smithsonian looking like some sort of possessed octopus as his hands moved with the speed of light between documents, feeding himself and writing notes.

As he wrote various notes, Mr. P continued to smile and immediately write a reply to Smithsonian on 3 x 5 cards. This, Zeke presumed, would be to have organized notes for the trial.

"Okay, let's see here – Mr. P writes and says 'We are excited about your case . . . ah, we hope it goes well . . . and that we will be going . . . .ah to . . . put something, something . . . ' and something about a rice bowl. I think."

Zeke was puzzled as Smithsonian tried to translate for Mr. P. At that moment Zeke began to ponder searching for a new law firm, but he couldn't argue with their success. Maybe their method was to confuse people so much that no one wanted to spend the time engaging them in court. But with over four hundred court cases successfully won, he had to trust that what they were doing was right.

After the meeting, Smithsonian set up a court date for the trial. He wanted to get an early date so the state would have little time to prepare.

As Malaysia headed home for the evening, she received a call from Zeke on her cell phone as she pulled out of the parking lot.

"Malaysia, can you head back to the office and print out that document you're working on, and bring it over to my house? I think they did something to the firewall and the email bounced. You know, the one I tried to email to my home address?"

Malaysia acknowledged Zeke's concerns and returned back to the office. As she pulled up to the building she hurried toward the front door. She slid her ID badge against the security scanner but could see the door was slightly ajar. She pushed the door open and could hear some scuffling in the back room. Malaysia's heart began to race – could this be the same gorilla, or man, that had attacked her previously? As she had previously suspected, it was probably Phil Speakeasy from Director Waxhead's office. She thought for a moment, took a deep breath and gathered her courage. Since the attack, she had taken judo classes and decided she wasn't going to let anyone intimidate her again.

She quietly snuck into the office and walked toward the back room. She could hear the intruder going through the filing cabinet. Light was bouncing off the walls as if a flashlight was being used. Without hesitation, Malaysia pounced. She leapt like a cat striking the intruder with the full force of her expensive Italian leather boot. The man went sailing into the wall in a heap of papers he had removed from the filing cabinet. He began to moan, and Malaysia knew she had knocked him semi-unconscious. She quickly brushed herself off and felt around the darkened wall for the light switch. She quickly illuminated the back-room only to be surprised by the identity of the intruder – Jimmy Tinzdale.

"Jimmy! What in the world are you doing here?" Malaysia said frantically. She ran over to Jimmy and helped him up.

Jimmy, still in somewhat of a haze tried to explain what

he was doing there. "Ah, I just needed some old reports, that's all."

"But why were you looking for them in the dark with a flashlight?"

"Look, Malaysia, why don't you mind your own business? I can do whatever I want!'

Malaysia looked at the file that Jimmy was grasping and noted it was Zeke's recent traffic study. "So you are here after hours and apparently need Zeke's traffic study?"

"Like I said, it's none of your business." Jimmy then turned to walk toward the front door.

"Hey, you can't just leave without an explanation, Jimmy!"

"Oh can't I? Just watch me!"

Malaysia ran over to Jimmy and tried to grab him by the arm. Jimmy swung his arm at her, forcing her back. As Jimmy reached for the door handle, he could feel Malaysia grabbing him from behind. He turned and swung his fist at Malaysia but badly missed as she quickly dropped to the ground. As Malaysia hit the floor she kicked at Jimmy's knee, knocking him to the floor in agony. Jimmy tried to regain his composure and grabbed at the file that had flown from his hand. As he reached for it, Malaysia dug her high-heeled shoe into his hand – which immediately resulted in a high-pitched scream from Jimmy.

"What's wrong, Jimmy? Can't take playing a little rough?"

Jimmy's ire, which was already used to being up, was now really up. He got up and charged at Malaysia. She dodged him like a matador narrowly escaping a mad bull.

Jimmy's head went straight into the wall, knocking him unconscious. Malaysia spotted some duct tape and bound Jimmy with it. She called the police and hoped they would arrive quickly. The news of Jimmy breaking into the office files was big, and she wanted to alert Zeke as soon as possible.

Before she could dial Zeke on her cell-phone, bright lights from outside of the office temporarily blinded her. It was a car pulling up to the building. She quickly drug Jimmy into the back-room and peered around the corner to see what was going on. She could make out a car and a dark figure slowly getting out of the driver's side. He had the height and the build of someone she was familiar with – Phil Speakeasy the "Gorilla Man."

In the back-room Malaysia could hear Jimmy moaning. She ripped off a piece of duct-tape and stuck it over his mouth. She waited quietly as she could hear the man pushing the front door open. This was no time to panic. It was time to be in control.

With all the confidence she could muster, Malaysia ran toward the front door and, as she had done previously with Jimmy, leapt into the air with all the fury of an enraged intellectual. As with Jimmy, she caught the man completely off-guard and sent him careening into the wall. She turned on the light and it was whom she expected to see – Speakeasy. With the look of a gold medalist from the Olympics, Malaysia stood triumphantly over Speakeasy. She then broke down into a schoolgirl giggle, relieved at what had happened. This time she had won, and the bad guys got their due.

As she bound Speakeasy with duct tape, the police pulled into the parking lot. Malaysia quickly informed the officers of what had happened and they took the two men into custody.

On the phone Malaysia was giving Zeke a quick rundown of what had happened and told him he would be over to his house in fifteen minutes. She felt good. Not only had she helped Zeke in his case against the state, but she had regained some confidence in herself that had been lacking. She could now take on the world again – like she had done at NASA. And maybe it was time for her to move on. Surely it was time to put her talents and intellect to good use. The next day she applied for a position at NASA – 'Astronaut Person' – at least that's what she put on her application anyway.

Several weeks later the trial date arrived. Zeke threw on a coat and tie and jumped into his truck to head over to the state courthouse. He was nervous, and wasn't sure what he was up against. The only thing he knew was this was important, and lives depended on him doing the right thing.

After parking in a nearby lot, he ran across the street and up the stairs leading to the courthouse. There at the front door he saw Malaysia.

"Go get 'em, Zeke. We're counting on you."

Zeke stopped and stared at Malaysia. She was her beautiful self and had a rather coy smile on her face. It was the look that he had dreamed about often.

"Thanks, Malaysia. Are you staying?"

"Ah, no. I just wanted to wish you luck."

Zeke was silent, a bit shy, not sure what to do or say. "Thanks, Malaysia. You know I couldn't have gotten this far without you."

They both smiled as Zeke grabbed the handle to the door. He turned for a final look at Malaysia. She blew him a soft and sultry kiss. Lucky for him Gloria was inside the courtroom.

Zeke ran like a crazy man down the hallway that led to the courtroom. There was a security check with metal detector that he had to go through. Once the check was completed he ran through the main doors to the courtroom. He quickly spotted his attorney Fred Smithsonian going through some files. He waved and smiled to Gloria as he took his seat next to Smithsonian.

"Geez, Zeke, like to cut it close don't you?" said Smithsonian. "Try and get to these things on time, okay?

Zeke smiled, and nodded to the affirmative.

"All rise. The most honorable Harry Hobblestone will preside."

The judge, with the appearance of a learned and educated magistrate, quickly slammed his gavel.

"The court is now in session. Mr. Smithsonian, do you have any opening comments?"

"Yes, your honor."

Smithsonian practically stumbled as he made his way toward the bench. Smithsonian was young and it was partly because of his inexperience that he had teamed up with Mr. P –they both needed each other.

"Your honor, we would like to make an opening statement." Smithsonian meekly looked over at Judge

Hobblestone who nodded his head and motioned for him to continue.

"We bring this case before you today to show that the state of Minnesota, in the form of former Director of Transportation, Dean Langhorn and his successor Harry Waxhead, did so conspire to alter the traffic laws in the state of Minnesota to the point where the average driver has been rendered incompetent when it comes to basic merging techniques."

"I object!" shouted Milton Mindwarp. Mindwarp was the defense attorney for the state of Minnesota. He received his undergraduate degree from the University of Minnesota and received his law degree online from the University of Berlin in Germany. No one was quite sure how he passed the bar, as his course work was entirely in German which he did not speak. Not to mention the course only covered German law.

"What grounds, Mr. Mindwarp?"

"This is pure speculation and hearsay, your honor."

"I'll be the judge of that," the judge said. "Please continue, Mr. Smithsonian."

"Yes, your honor. We will show that time and time again that Langhorn and Waxhead altered the traffic laws in Minnesota to create more accidents to which they would receive kickbacks from large towing companies. It is in fact the reason why Minnesota leads all other states in the amount of towing companies per capita. We will also show gross negligence on their part to not properly update roads and streets in such a way that on-ramps and off-ramps became so confusing that again traffic accidents were not prevented but were assured of happening."

As Smithsonian turned toward the audience he became motionless. At the back of the courtroom coming through the door was his ex-wife Stella. Stella was wearing a black suit with short skirt and black stockings with high-heels. Yes, she was to die for. Part of the reason why Smithsonian was now working for Mr. P was because his ex-wife had got everything in their divorce proceedings. She was the true definition of a "Devil in a Blue Dress," or in this case, short black skirt, black stockings and high heels.

Whatever the reason for her appearance in the courtroom, Smithsonian froze. He began to shake a little, and then sweat began to form on his brow and soon on the rest of his face and body. Waxhead had truly done his homework.

"Ah, Mr. Smithsonian . . . are you done with your opening remarks?" the judge queried.

Smithsonian stood there like a stone. It quickly became an uncomfortable silence, with the courtroom beginning to murmur. Zeke tried to tug at Smithsonian's sleeve to get him to snap out of it.

"Mr. Smithsonian? Mr. Smithsonian, are you okay?"

Just as it seemed all had turned dark, Mr. P arrived at the doorway.

"WHORE EVERY DINK!!!" Mr. P cried.

Everyone in the courtroom turned to look at Mr. P. An embarrassed Zeke rose to his feet and tried to explain to the judge what he thought Mr. P meant to say.

"I think he means hold everything, your honor," Zeke said with caution in his voice.

"No, I mean – SHE IS A WHORE!!!" Mr. P pointed over

to Smithsonian's ex-wife.

With that Mr. P ran down the aisle way and was greeted by a truly thankful Zeke. Mr. P tried to relax Smithsonian who finally broke from his statue impersonation. Mr. P talked with Smithsonian and finally got him to settle down and focus.

"Mr. Smithsonian, are you okay?"

"Ah, yes, your honor . . . ah, just had a bit of a fright." Smithsonian pulled out a handkerchief and began to dab the gallon of sweat that had formed on his head.

"Mr. Smithsonian, who is this gentleman that has joined you?'

Smithsonian went on to explain who Mr. P was. Judge Hobblestone was sympathetic to Mr. P's plight and welcomed him to the courtroom. Hobblestone had been a fighter pilot during the Vietnam War and had been shot down near the border between Thailand and Laos. There he lived for years on mountain scrubs and ferns. He later found a village where its inhabitants pronounced him king and he ruled with love and kindness as the villagers showered him with durians, moonshine and concubines. If it were not for the fact that his brother had launched a massive man-hunt and dragged him back to the United States in 1983, Judge Hobblestone, or King Hobblestone, would still be ruling a small Thai village to this day. Needless to say, Judge Hobblestone had a fondness for all things Thai and Southeast Asian.

"Mr. Smithsonian, or Mr. Prahnpratvinchalnuralpravin, would you like to call your first witness?" The judge pronounced Mr. P's name with surprising accuracy.

"Yes, your honor. We'd like to call Zeke Martin to the stand."

People gasped as Zeke's name was called, having no idea who Zeke was. Zeke slowly approached the stand, raised his hand and took the oath.

"Do you swear to tell the truth, the whole truth and nothing but the truth?"

"I do" quivered Zeke, staring at the judge to see if it was okay to sit down.

Both Smithsonian and Mr. P approached Zeke. It was almost like Mr. P was Smithsonian's shadow, he followed him so closely.

"Now, Mr. Martin, how long have you been in the Burnsville office of the Department of Transportation?"

"That will be twenty years next month."

"Objection!" Mindwarp screamed at the top of his lungs.

"Mindwarp, you're not going to start this again are you, like your last trial?"

"Your honor, the length of Zeke Martin's tenure in the Burnsville office has nothing to do with the trial."

The judge looked wearily over to Smithsonian.

"You honor, we are merely trying to establish that Zeke Martin is a seasoned professional in the Department of Transportation."

It was going to be a long trail. Mindwarp was known for his belligerent approach and his continuous objections which slowed things down and would frustrate the prosecution.

After getting through Zeke's background, Smithsonian walked Zeke through various events surrounding the case, including his videotape studies which showed ABC towing trucks in the background, the department's holiday party and the Waxhead's cabin. After several hours of testimony and Mindwarp's objections, Smithsonian deferred to Mindwarp.

"Your witness," a more confident Smithsonian said to Mindwarp, with Mr. P in close pursuit.

"Mr. Martin sir, are you familiar with statute 41-B389C24 of the State Manual for Traffic Laws and Addendums?"

"Yes, I am," Zeke said assuredly.

The unconvinced lawyer turned away from Zeke with his arms folded, thinking of how he could trap his ignorant prey. "Have you heard of statute 53-71Z2TF?!!!"

"Yes!" Zeke immediately shot back to the surprised attorney.

Again the truculent lawyer pulled away. He immediately retaliated . . ."Statute 101-6543.24ABCD?"

"Yes!"

"Statute 5010-BYZ853. Stoke 12?"

"Yes!"

"5218ABZY-536?"

"Yes."

"7H815 . . ."

"Yes!"

"Mr. Mindwarp, is there a particular line of reasoning you are attempting to take with this litany of statutes?"

"Yes, your honor, I am attempting to establish that Mr. Martin, as an outsider to Minnesota, has no concept of state laws and statutes."

"And are you being successful so far?"

"Well, your honor, let's find out. Mr. Martin . . . what does statute 41-B389C24 say?"

Zeke thought to himself for a moment. He hesitated but then began to speak. "I believe statute 41-B389C24 says that all sign posts shall be clearly visible and not restricted by foliage, buildings, other sign posts, livestock, clowns, etc . . ."

The lawyer again crossed his arms and began to pace in front of Zeke. He turned and shouted back at Zeke. "Foliage, Mr. Martin! What does foliage mean to you?"

"Objection, your honor!" Smithsonian jumped to his feet with the most pained facial expression two years of acting school could muster.

"Yes, counselor," the judge mumbled back, fantasizing to himself about the plate of turkey and mashed potatoes he would be having down at Jimmy's as soon as he felt it necessary to adjourn.

"Your honor, it is obvious that the prosecutor is clearly . . . ah . . . clearly . . ."

"Yes."

"Clearly, uh . . . uh, leading the witness!"

"Leading the witness where?"

"Uh, I don't know . . . somewhere?"

The judge rolled his eyes, wondering what law school the latest crop of attorneys were coming from these days.

"Actually, I'll object for you. Mr. Mindwarp, what are you now trying to establish . . . that the defendant does not have a clear understanding of the definition of foliage?"

"Clearly, your honor, for a man to hold such a high position as Mr. Martin, he must know this statute inside and out. I'm merely trying to show that Mr. Martin has a limited understanding of these statutes and therefore unworthy of such a high post."

The judge shook his head, stared up at the ceiling and then let out a sigh. He motioned for Mindwarp to continue.

"Mr. Martin, what type of other sign posts cannot be placed in front of sign posts with regard to statute 41-B389C24?"

"I suppose any signpost that would impede the driver from seeing the other signpost."

The lawyer did the obligatory arms-folded march-away from Zeke. In almost the same time span as previous, the lawyer made his already well-known staged movement – raising his index finger to his cheek, turning and then railing the plaintiff. His three years of modeling school had not paid off.

"You *suppose*?" he said with a feigned look of agitation. "Not that 'you know that' . . . but you '*suppose*'?"

The crowd looked at one another in hushed astonishment, unsure as to why they were looking at each other in hushed astonishment. The judge, already tired of Mindwarp, and knowing any objection was going to take the interrogation passed the three hour mark, sighed in disbelief. Mindwarp took this to mean the judge was highly impressed. He smiled and nodded to the prosecution table and the crowd behind them. He winked at a young woman that had come solely to view the well-known prosecutor in action.

"Supposing is quite different from knowing isn't it, Mr. Martin?"

"Yes, I suppose it is."

The judge slapped himself in the forehead trying to keep his composure from Zeke's obvious slip of the tongue. He could only conceive of where Mindwarp would take it now.

"You SUPPOS-S-S-S-S-S-S-SE, about supposing?!!!" Mindwarp again turned to the crowd with a large, sparkling smile.

The crowd collectively held their breaths in anticipation. When they could not collectively come up with a reason why they should hold their breaths, they sighed a collective sigh of relief. The prosecutor pulled a handkerchief from his top suit pocket and dabbed the produce of the collective sigh of relief from his brow. He returned to pick up the assault.

"You sound very unsure of yourself, Mr. Martin."

"Well, I mean I never memorize the State Manual for Traffic Laws and Addendums."

Again the audience gasped, this time with many of the members actually understanding why they were gasping.

"I see . . . you never thought that worthwhile enough to memorize?"

The lawyer walked around liked a caged cat with its arms folded, with one hand on its cheek, wearing an expensive Italian suit.

"Mr. Mindwarp, I know it may seem hard to believe, but many people do not memorize every single aspect, word and letter of their job requirements," the judge said with clenched teeth, while the crowd again gasped. "It does not conclude or even imply that Mr. Martin is incompetent by not memorizing the State Manual for Traffic Laws and Addendums. And I will warn the entire courtroom to refrain from gasping any further or they shall be removed!"

The audience tried collectively not to gasp, looking around quietly for any offenders of the new gasping restriction that had been placed on them.

The attorney, puzzled by the judge's lack of support, began to give the judge the "evil-eye" to which the judge blinked several times and then stared him down until the lawyer turned away in a huff.

"Mr. Smithsonian, call your next witness please."

"Harry Steel to the stand please."

The crowd gasped in silence as the chief of ABC Towing and the head of the Towing industry stood and walked toward the stand. Rising along with Smithsonian was Mr. P who accompanied him to the stand. The judge had a curious look on his face as both men approached the witness stand where Harry Steel now sat.

"If your honor would allow, Mr. Prahnprat-vinchalnuralpravin would like to examine the witness."

The judge, with a look like he had seen everything, waved his hand to continue.

Mr P approached Harry Steel and stared at him. Steel, not to mention everyone in the courthouse, was a little uncomfortable with the long stare.

"Mistuh Steel, you big . . . how you say boss, no?"

Steel shrugged his shoulders, not sure what kind of response Mr. P wanted.

"You have powa, sir. You big boss wiv powa, sir!"

"What's powa?"

"Mr. Prahnpratvinchalnuralpravin is saying the word power," said Smithsonian.

The courtroom burst into laughter, unable to control the humor from Mr. P's broken English.

"Alright, quiet down. How would you like it if you were from another country?!!!" yelled an angry Smithsonian. "How would you like it if you grew up in a dangerous region in Southeast Asia?"

Smithsonian paused for effect.

"Yah, well, that's what happened to Mr. Prahnpratvinchalnuralpravin, or who we affectionately refer to as Mr. P."

Several young boys burst into laughter after hearing about Mr. P's moniker.

"How would have liked to have subsisted on nothing but grass and bugs for eight years? How would you have liked to have crawled on your belly for eighteen miles to sneak away from a drug-lord's prison? How many of you can say you have done that?"

Slowly several hands were raised. Smithsonian with a skeptical look on his face walked toward the aisle.

"Oh really? And how many of you came to this country not knowing a word of English and dirt poor?"

Slowly about three quarters of the courtroom raised their hands. Smithsonian rolled his eyes and turned to look for the judge in support.

"Sorry, Smithsonian, but half our courtroom is filled with Colombian or Mung refugees looking for a little entertainment."

Smithsonian turned back to the crowd.

"Then of all peoples you should respect a man like Mr. P. Why do you laugh at such a distinguished man? A self-made man who moved his entire family from Thailand to the United States, a man who has helped support his parents, siblings, aunts and uncles and even distant relatives and friends. This is a man to be admired!"

With Smithsonian choking back tears, the entire crowd gave a ten-minute standing ovation for Mr. P. It was like a scene from the Lou Gehrig story . . . except it wasn't about baseball, or at a baseball park. Mr. P basked in the love that the courtroom was showering him with. He beamed, completely unaware of why the crowd was applauding. Smithsonian raised his hands to have the crowd stop.

"Continue Mr. P," Smithsonian said as he placed his hand onto his shoulder.

"Mistuh Steel, wot is u rangemint wit ahhari Wexed?"

Again the confused courtroom burst into laughter. Smithsonian shook his head, hating each and every member of the crowd.

"I don't think I understand the question," a confused Harry Steel said.

"I think what Mr. Prahnpratvinchalnuralpravin . . . ah Mr. P wants to know is the nature of your relationship or arrangements you might have with Harry Waxhead," Said Smithsonian.

"Well, it's purely personal. We are good friends. Our families are quite close and we often vacation together."

Mr. P nodded and began to pace back and forth in front of Steel. "Mistah Steel . . . is not these fendchip mowed dan jista fendchip?"

A puzzled Harry Steel looked to Smithsonian for an interpretation.

"Mr. P is asking if your friendship is something more than just friendship?"

"You mean are we gay?"

"No, he means like do you have a business relationship as well?"

Steel was quiet and looked over at Waxhead who immediately shook his head. All eyes turned to both men as they exchanged glances, and then made weird faces that seemed to convey hidden messages.

"Our relationship is entirely . . . uh copasetic."

"Copasetic?" Smithsonian queried.

"You know . . . menial."

"Menial?"

"You know . . . what's the word?"

"I'm not sure."

"You know, the word, the word that means that you do not have a business partnership of any kind including a corporation or LLP or LLC?"

"Can't you just say you don't have a business partnership of any kind with Mr. Waxhead?"

Mr. Steel looked puzzled. "Ah, sure . . . why not?" he said, shrugging his shoulders and smiling at the judge.

The courtroom audience began to laugh at Mr. Steel's grasp of the English language which appeared to be about as thorough as Mr. P's. Mr. P then walked over to Smithsonian and whispered in his ear. Smithsonian nodded as he listened. Mr. P then smiled and walked toward Steel.

"Mr. Steel, there is an old Thai expression that says that a monkey cannot just be friends with a mango – it has to consume the mango."

Steel stared at Smithsonian, hoping desperately that he would finish the expression – but there was no further explanation forthcoming.

"Are you saying, do I consume Harry Waxhead?"

"Ah, just a second." Smithsonian walked back to Mr. P who again whispered in his ear.

"There is a saying in Thailand that goes like this. When a monkey and a mango and a full-moon are present . . . no that's not it." Again Smithsonian walked back to a frustrated Mr. P who again whispered into his ear.

"Okay, when a monkey throws a mango at the moon someone's uncle is about to get it . . ." Smithsonian looked back at Mr. P who was frantically shaking his head.

Zeke looked at the proceedings before him and wondered if someone had slipped him a tab of LSD. Clearly this was a scene seldom seen in any court of law. But of course we are talking about people here, and anything was possible when human beings are involved.

"I think I finally have it. Mr. Steel, it is said in Thailand that when a monkey and a cobra meet it's not for friendship."

"Are you calling me a monkey?" an agitated Mr. Steel complained.

"Ah no. It's just that in Thailand when a monkey meets a cobra . . . ah . . . they . . ."

Again Smithsonian looked to Mr. P for help. Mr. P leaning over the prosecution's table tried to whisper to him. He was leaning to the point to where no one was quite sure how he could keep from falling – he was definitely challenging the laws of physics.

" . . . when a monkey and a cobra meet . . . it's usually for business."

"I'll be a monkey's uncle!" the judge muttered to himself.

"I'm not understanding you?" Steel said, with a pained look on his face.

"Oh I bet you do," Smithsonian said, with a confident smile and then turned toward the jury. "I bet you do. No further questions, your honor."

When Mindwarp refused to question Steel, Judge Hobblestone asked Smithsonian for his next witness.

"We would like to call to the stand Harry Waxhead."

Waxhead looked around the courtroom with a paranoid expression on his face. He straightened his tie and rose to his feet. The courtroom was hushed as they peered upon the man who quite possibly had the entire state of Minnesota brainwashed. He closed his eyes for a moment, then walked confidently to the stand and took the oath. Waxhead now looked calm and collected, ready to take any question they could throw at him.

Smithsonian walked slowly toward Waxhead with some papers he was flipping through. He handed them to Waxhead.

"Mr. Waxhead, do these invoices look familiar to you?"

Waxhead searched through the many pieces of paper, shaking his head like he had no clue what they were.

"Ah, no, I've never seen these before in my life."

Smithsonian walked away from Waxhead toward the courtroom and began to look skyward.

"I see . . . you've never seen these invoices before in your life? Well you are probably correct because these invoices came from ABC Towing Company and were sent to the state's accounts payable department. These were promptly paid with no one inspecting them at all. No one inspecting them at all because you advised accounts payable to pay anything that ABC Towing submitted, didn't you, Mr. Waxhead?"

Waxhead's jaw dropped. He began to shake like he was on some sort of vibrating chair.

"That's preposterous! I would never authorize anything like that! Anyway, the state would audit any charges."

"They may audit them, but if the charges are legitimate there's nothing much they can do about it. Correct?"

"Yah, so?"

"So the whole point is that you hired ABC Towing knowing how the system was inherently set up to create accidents and thereby provide ABC Towing with a large income. An income in fact that made them a Fortune 1000 company – making over one billion dollars each year. And the number-one stock holder in the company is Harry Waxhead."

"So you can't fault me for investing – it's not against the law!"

"No, but gross negligence is against the law! We will prove that you conspired to create a system whereby the good citizens of Minnesota were duped into not applying the proper merging techniques, whereby they have become the drivers most prone to create accidents. The mere fact that ABC Towing is a billion dollar a year enterprise proves that fact. The next leading Towing Company outside the state is Fred's Towing of Manhattan, New York who made

$339,000 last year picking up stranded motorists!"

Waxhead looked uneasy. He produced a handkerchief from his suit jacket and began to dab his forehead. Smithsonian went to his briefcase and pulled out a thick manual. He walked over to Waxhead and tossed it into his lap.

"Mr. Waxhead, can I get you to read me the name of the manual that I've placed into your lap?"

Waxhead knew what it was but pretended to fumble with it like it was some foreign object he didn't have a clue what it was.

"Ah, well, it says it's the Federal Manual for State Traffic Laws."

"Yes, Mr. Waxhead, that is correct. Can you please turn to page 736?"

Waxhead again began to fumble around with the gangly large book as if were the Yellow Pages.

"Yes, I found it."

"Could you please read to the court what section 5, article B6 says?"

"Ah, it says that local states are responsible for the enforcement and proper training of drivers with regard to the proper merging techniques."

Smithsonian was silent. He then walked back to his table and retrieved another large manual – again as before he tossed the large book into Waxhead's lap.

"All right, Mr. Waxhead, as you can see and as you are probably familiar with, this manual is the State Manual for Traffic Laws and Addendums. Now will you kindly turn to page 983, section 12 D?"

Waxhead knew what Smithsonian was doing, but played along, finally arriving at the page.

"Ah, there is no section 12D."

"Precisely!" Smithsonian yelled, making Waxhead and the rest of the courtroom jump.

"I object!" yelled an equally perturbed Mindwarp.

"What grounds, counselor?"

"On the grounds he's leading the witness."

"Overruled. Continue, Mr. Smithsonian."

"Thank you, your honor. You are precisely correct, Mr. Waxhead. And why is it there is no section 12D? Well, every other state in the union has a section 12D. And, Mr. Waxhead, do you know what 12D reads? I am sure you do!"

Waxhead shook his head like he had no clue what Smithsonian meant.

"12D reads as follows. 'Each driver shall be trained on the correct merging procedures. A driver shall first check the lane he or she is planning to merge to, checking to the left or right, then looking over their shoulder to spot any traffic. They shall then place their turn signal in the direction of their turn, check their side-view mirror and then proceed to merge in a smooth and gradual fashion into the next lane.'"

Smithsonian with a large grin on his face began to pace in front of Waxhead. Waxhead was sweating and had a panicked look on his face. He knew the hammer was about to fall.

"So, Mr. Waxhead, my question to you, and the question that the entire state of Minnesota poses to you, is this . . ."

The crowd looked on in complete silence waiting for the question to be posed. People were on the edge of their seats in near gasp and doing everything they could to muffle their gasps as the court had previously ordered.

"WHY?! WHY, MR. WAXHEAD?! WHY does the 'State Traffic Laws and Addendums' manual not have a section 12D?"

Waxhead twisted and turned in his chair.

"May I remind the witness that he is in a court of law and . . ."

With that, a nervous Harry Waxhead bolted from the witness stand and quickly ran past Smithsonian, sending him careening into Mr. P. Waxhead ran past two guards at the doorway who looked like they had been immobilized. The audience was in an uproar and the judge began to bang his gavel. Zeke looked toward Gloria who nodded toward the doorway. Zeke knew what he needed to do.

CHAPTER 11

Zeke ran across the street to the parking lot where he had left his truck. He slammed the key into the ignition and quickly moved the gear shift into reverse. Everyone could hear the squeal from Zeke's tires as he floored the gas pedal. Dust and smoke rose in a great funnel along with thousands of candy wrappers and a host of other miscellaneous debris.

Zeke caught eye of Waxhead's BMW as he zoomed onto 35W toward South St. Paul and the Mississippi Bridge. Like a wild chase from a police detective movie, Zeke zipped in and out of traffic trying to catch up with Waxhead. Waxhead had a souped-up BMW with a .457 engine and dual overhead fuel-injection draft winglets that made that baby fly. It was all Zeke could do to keep up in his '57 Ford pick-up.

Waxhead laughed as he eyed Zeke in his rearview mirror. He knew Zeke wouldn't be able to keep up with him, and immediately floored the gas pedal.

As Zeke veered in and out of traffic, his cell phone began to ring. It was Gloria.

"Zeke, are you okay?" she almost screamed.

"Yes, honey, I am."

Gloria was quiet. It had been years since she had heard the word "honey," and it sounded good.

"I love you, Zeke! Please be careful."

"I will, honey. I love you too."

"Zeke?"

"Yes, honey?"

"What would you like for dinner tonight?"

"Uh . . . I'll talk to you later. Bye."

With that, Zeke threw the cell phone down on the passenger side and began to zero in on Waxhead. Before he knew it, they had reached the 494 freeway heading westbound. Zeke realized that they were averaging 100 miles per hour. He hoped the old truck could take it. Waxhead's BMW was hardly bearing any strain on the engine and could easily pick up more speed with a quick punch of the gas.

As the two speeded across the Mississippi toward the airport, Zeke began to wonder what might be Waxhead's intention. Did he have a plane waiting for him? What could be his plan be for heading over to Bloomington?

As they raced toward the airport, Zeke became alarmed with the amount of traffic that was starting to build up. He glanced at his watch and could see it was the beginnings of rush hour. Now Minnesota Merging would really be put to the test.

If there was one thing that Zeke had learned for all the years he had been in Minnesota, it was how to anticipate when a Minnesotan was about to merge. He could see the panicked looks on people's faces as they turned to look back into the lane they wanted – that was a quick clue that he didn't want to go in that direction. He would quickly fly around these people and end up in the lane ahead of them.

Weaving in and out of traffic no longer became an option as they neared the airport. Waxhead was now near the Mall of Minnesota off of Cedar. Zeke came to a halt near the 24th Avenue exit. There was only one course of action for Zeke. With all of his concern for Minnesota drivers, it was perhaps their technique of merging three miles ahead of time that might actually help him. As he eyed the far right lane, he could see that it was open for miles. He immediately accelerated into the right lane and began to zoom back down the freeway.

He could see in the distance that Waxhead had been held up, and now was his chance. Zeke gunned the engine. He was almost upon Waxhead when he could see the right lane coming to an end, and a sign blaring "Merge" was almost upon him.

"Hey, where do you think you are going, you Son of a #$%^&*?" screamed one occupant from his Dodge Neon.

Zeke ignored the rumblings of the cars that were almost bumper to bumper. As he began to slow to merge, he could see the front end of another car start to pull over to the far right lane. It was an elderly man who had spotted Zeke coming and was not about to let him merge this late in the process.

Zeke quickly swerved to miss him, but just then another car, a late model Mustang, also followed suit and nosed his car into the merging lane. Zeke forced his truck up the curb and onto some grass by the side of the freeway. As another car tried to come into that lane to block potential merging offenders, a gas truck running late had been tailing Zeke and immediately plowed into that car. An explosion ensued and Zeke just missed a fireball.

He floored the gas pedal and turned onto the Cedar southbound that would go right back over the 494 westbound lane. He followed Waxhead who had taken the same exit. Zeke was right behind Waxhead on the loop that would put them onto the southbound lane of Cedar.

As Zeke drove over the overpass that would lead to the Mall of Minnesota, he could see the freeway ablaze below him. He hoped that no one was hurt, but given the massive explosion that was unlikely. The two cars barreled down the off-ramp that led directly to the Mall of Minnesota.

Waxhead drove quickly up the street that led to the multi-level parking lot at the mall. Zeke then chased Waxhead into the top level of parking near the Harrington's anchor store. Waxhead squealed to a stop and immediately ran into the mall. Zeke was in quick pursuit behind him. As the two men raced through the store, Zeke decided to stop at one of the check-out stands.

"Miss, I need your help?"

"Oh yes, sir, I know what kind of help you need. You need to fill out an application for a new Harrington's credit card and get twenty percent off on your next purchase."

"No, no. I need you to call the security supervisor right now!"

The young girl's expression immediately turned to panic, but she did exactly as Zeke instructed.

Soon a security detail was dispatched and met Zeke at the store's entrance to the mall.

"Okay, boys, we have a dangerous guy on the loose in here. We need to shut down the mall and put security at each entrance."

"Got it, and uh, who are you?" said one confused guard.

"I'm Zeke Martin. I'm with the Department of Transportation."

The mall's security chief eyed him up and down, wondering why he was taking instructions from someone from the Department of Transportation. He decided he had nothing better to do.

"Okay, men, fan out . . . ah, what does this guy look like?"

"He's in his late fifties, bald, wears glasses and is wearing a very tacky black suit and tie."

"Got it! Let's go, men!"

Zeke began a frantic run through the mall trying to figure out where Waxhead would hide. He made a quick sweep of every store in the MOM which was no easy task. He was relying heavily on his football experience which helped him to weave in and out of store displays, coat racks, bins and various other sundry merchandising set-ups.

"Have you seen anything?" Zeke cried out to the security chief who had made a sweep from the opposite end of the mall.

"No, no luck. I have men on the second and third floors as well, and they haven't seen anything."

Just then Zeke saw a flash in his peripheral vision – Waxhead had run into the Elizabeth's Hidden Agenda –

Ladies Intimate Apparel. Zeke raced into the store after him and immediately came to a halt. This was the largest store he had ever seen where ladies' intimates were publicly displayed. His eyes began to roam over the inventory, fantasizing about both Gloria and Malaysia modeling some of the naughtier items. He began to think that he should have been buying Gloria some of these undergarments over the years to spice up their relationship, but he had often heard that it was something that was more selfish for the man rather than being thoughtful for the woman. Anyway, it wasn't time to be thinking about teddies and panties and stockings and garters. It was time to catch a criminal!

Zeke began to scour around the various racks of clothing that were held up, almost taunting his masculinity. He began to shake his head. This was the worst store in the entire MOM that Waxhead could have chosen.

"Get a hold of yourself, Martin!" Zeke practically slapped himself in the face as he tried to clear his head.

He noticed some ruffling amongst a rack of lacey bras. He began to work his way through the rack but was soon tangled up in the straps. As he pushed away the sea of breast support, he could see what appeared to be Waxhead in the center of the clothing rack.

"All right, Waxhead, the jig is up!"

Before Zeke knew what hit him, Waxhead bolted out of an opening in the rack and disappeared. Zeke, still tangled up in the bras became even more twisted and caught with each swipe he took. It was like the Amazon of bras. He had no other choice but to quickly grab his pocket knife. He prided himself on the Swiss Army knife that he took with him everywhere. Whether he was camping or fishing, or trying to free himself from ladies undergarments, the Swiss Army knife never failed. He immediately attacked the beastly brassieres, slaying them with quick hacks of the largest blade. He was soon free and ran to the front of the entrance of the store.

Zeke linked up with the MOM's security chief who told him that all of the stores were clear. Zeke's jaw dropped. He knew what that meant. The only possible place that Waxhead could have gone to was to the amusement park in the middle of the mall. For Zeke that would be frightening. The two things that he feared the most were merging in Minnesota, and amusement parks. There was something always in the back of his mind when he got on a ride – would the darn thing come off the tracks and crash? He enjoyed the engineering aspects of the amusement parks, but he didn't want to be the one trying out someone else's designs. But at this point, the safety of the public was at risk and he needed to find Waxhead.

The amusement park in the MOM was based on the original comic characters of Stanley Martz –The Pecans. The Pecans were lovable cartoon characters featuring such beloved characters as Smiley Smith, Bonnie the Brat, Silly Sally and Sophocles. Smiley had an adorable pet Basset Hound named Droopy (because of his eyes) who went around pretending he was Mario Andretti driving his doghouse in mock versions of the Indianapolis 500. He always blew out a tire in the end, and so never won.

As Zeke cruised around Camp Droopy, he thought he could see Waxhead darting in and out of various rides. He soon spotted him making a run for the Log Shoot. As Waxhead entered the Log Shoot he knocked down the attendant and threw the lever for the ride to accelerate. He hopped into one of the open log rides and turned to scoff at Zeke. Zeke immediately ran up to the attendant to see if he was okay. He then jumped into the next log boat and was in hot pursuit.

At the first part of the ride the log boats were carried up what seemed like an endless stream, with water rushing all around the boats. The conveyer belt sound underneath the boat was the only thing that let the passenger know they were attached to anything. As the boats climbed up the stream at a distinct incline they soon entered a large cave. The cave had the appearance of a mine shaft with all the equipment and tools that would accompany a miner from the turn of the nineteenth century.

As the two men's boat climbed higher and higher into the mine, Zeke decided to try and climb out of his boat and either jump onto Waxhead's boat or onto the ceramic cave floor immediately to the sides of the flume that was carrying the boats. As Zeke began to perch himself at the front of the boat for a jump, he could see his and Waxhead's boats nearing the top of the mine shaft. He could also hear the sound of roaring water as it cascaded down a waterfall.

Zeke made a quick lunge for the back of Waxhead's boat as it reached the summit. Unfortunately, he fell short and could only manage to grab a hold of the back end of Waxhead's boat. He was clinging to the back of the boat as it roared over the top of the waterfall. Zeke was unsure of what to do: let go and fall into the water, possibly being sucked into the conveyor belt, or fly a hundred feet to his death.

Zeke didn't have time to think, and he was airborne with the log boat careening down the waterfall. He could feel his feet bouncing off the water as he and the boat raced toward the bottom. Within seconds he and the boat exploded into a giant water ball at the bottom of the ride. The force of the water sent Zeke into an artificial bush on the other side of a gate that separated the log ride from the rest of Camp Droopy. Zeke was dazed but had a moment of luck. Waxhead had enjoyed the ride so much that he stopped to purchase a picture of himself coming down the waterfall.

With a quick double-take Waxhead saw Zeke and began to run as fast as he could. Zeke was in hot pursuit but then lost Waxhead in the Ghost Ride. Zeke ran around in complete darkness, bumping into the odd gravestone and ghoul, but had no luck tracking down Waxhead. Where could he have escaped to?

Zeke wandered frantically around the dark hallways and mock graveyards of the Ghost Ride. Luckily for Zeke he found a clue – it was Waxhead's wallet. He must have dropped it near the exit to the Ghost Ride. Zeke ran out of the exit and back into the daylight of the MOM. He peered around in all directions but could not see anything . . . until he heard the uncontrolled laughter of what sounded like a madman. Off in the distance Zeke could see Waxhead running toward the far exit to Camp Droopy.

Zeke noticed a ride that had a gigantic tree with many swings attached underneath its branches. The tree would rotate around at fast speeds, providing a rather scary swing ride. Zeke motioned to the attendant to put the ride into operation and quickly hopped onto one of the swings. The swings were small seats dangling from long chains attached at the branches at the very top of the tree. You would secure yourself in the seat with a metal bar that would lower down to your waist.

Zeke decided he would not use the security bar. As the swing started to rotate, he began to lean off the edge of the seat. As the swing gained speed, Zeke waited for one more revolution. As he completed another 360 degrees of rotation, Zeke let go of the swing as it flung him over the center of Camp Droopy. He landed perfectly on top of Waxhead, sending the criminal sprawling into a pile of fake Pecan characters. Zeke was dazed, but pleased with his work. Waxhead was knocked unconscious, and the mall security was soon taking him into custody.

As Zeke left the MOM, he was immediately greeted by reporters.

"Mr. Martin, how do you feel about capturing Director Waxhead?"

"Well, I'm happy. I'm happy for the people of Minnesota. We can now have safe traffic laws that will allow people to drive without fear."

And it was true. Zeke was promoted to Director and began working with state legislators to redefine the state's traffic laws, and to begin programs all around the state on how to safely merge into and out of traffic. Zeke was pleased, and could now sleep at night.

The outpouring of gratitude from Minnesotans to Zeke was incredible, and the governor of the state made plans for a "Safe Driving Day" in Minnesota. Zeke was excited and was invited to speak in front of the capital building.

"Today we start a new day in Minnesota," Zeke said to a cheering crowd in front of the capital rotunda.

"No more will we drive unsafely. No more will we drive in ignorance! NO MORE WILL WE COMPROMISE THE WELL-BEING OF THE MINNESOTA MOTORIST!!!" Zeke pounded his fist onto a podium.

The audience stood and applauded uncontrollably as the governor grabbed Zeke by the hand, raising their fists skyward in triumph. The governor was next to speak.

"Dear citizens of Minnesota, you can now rest, knowing your director, Zeke Martin, is hard at work bringing you updated training and new tools that will allow you to drive safely and securely around our fair state.

"And now, we cut the ribbon over the new 35W bridge. The building of the bridge was sponsored of course by Malibou Coffee with over five hundred convenient locations around the country. Some of these locations are now equipped with drive-thrus to provide you with the most convenient service. And now to cut the ribbon is Malibou CEO Fred Wick!"

The opening of the new bridge was in combination with the hunting season opener. Arranged along with this would be anxious hunters and their families, waiting in their trucks and campers ready to race northward for the season-opener. As CEO Wick cut the ribbon, the impatient motorists revved their engines and immediately accelerated. What quickly ensued was the worst pile-up in Minnesota history. The governor looked over to Zeke and ordered him to start mandatory merging training first thing Monday morning for the entire state of Minnesota.

That Monday, Zeke applied for a new opening for assistant investigator in Birmingham Alabama. He knew when it was a good time to move on.

Made in the USA
Coppell, TX
19 July 2020